Carter's eyes looked bright and innocent in the semi-darkness. "What's wrong, Stacy?"

Silently she shook her head, trying to clear away the champagne bubbles. It was impossible to keep pretending she just enjoyed Carter's company and that was all. She knew perfectly well she wouldn't have responded to Carter's kiss if she wasn't . . .

"Stacy, what is it?" He broke into her thoughts urgently, his hands on her shoulders in a tight, demanding grip.

She stared up at him in total surprise. "I think I'm in love with you," she said in a dazed voice.

Other books in the **ROOMMATES** series:

COMING SOON

Roommates

TEACHER'S PET

Alison Blair

IVY BOOKS • NEW YORK

For Cynthia, Mimi, and Dara

Ivy Books
Published by Ballantine Books
Copyright © 1988 by Butterfield Press, Inc.

Produced by Butterfield Press, Inc.
133 Fifth Avenue
New York, New York 10003

Library of Congress Catalog Card Number: 87-90998

ISBN 0-8041-0064-0

Printed in Canada

First Edition: January 1988

Teacher's Pet

Chapter 1

Stacy Swanson took a step back from the clay-spattered workbench, and cocked her head to one side. She pursed her lips in concentration.

"Well?" she prompted anxiously. "What do you think?"

Her roommate, Maddie Lerner, looked up from her book and studied the ornate clay sculpture taking shape in front of Stacy. Wrinkling her nose, Maddie gave her friend a firm nod. "It's getting there."

"I don't know," Stacy countered. She pushed a lock of gleaming gold hair off her forehead with the back of one dirty hand, and let out a long, weary sigh. "Every time I touch it, it just seems to get worse."

Maddie shut her book with a snap, stood up,

1

and walked over to Stacy. "Listen, Stace," she said as she put a hand on Stacy's shoulder. "You've been working on this piece for a couple of weeks. Maybe you just need to take a break or something."

With another sigh, Stacy nodded, and sat down on a tall metal stool. The ceramics studio of Hawthorne College was beginning to feel more like a prison than a place for inspiration, she thought. She stared morosely at her half-finished sculpture, a wet, glistening mound of clay that refused to become what she wanted it to. No matter what angle she approached it from, she just could not make it turn out right.

She picked up a blob of wet, gooey clay and pounded it into a pancake on the workbench. "It's so hot in here," she whined in small, tired voice.

Maddie laughed. "Well, what do you expect from Georgia in the middle of July?"

"Yeah. You're right, I guess." Stacy shrugged, and rested her elbows on the workbench. "I'm beginning to think I shouldn't have stayed here for the whole summer. I must have been out of my mind to let you guys talk me into it."

There was a short silence, broken only by the faint *whirr* of the ceiling fan that barely stirred the humid air inside the studio. Stacy looked up at her friend's face. "Sorry, Mad. I'm just being a spoiled brat, as usual."

"Forget it. I know what you mean. It's much too hot, especially when you have to work," Maddie added.

For a moment, Stacy was tempted to say more. Ever since she and her three suitemates—Samantha Hill, Roni Davies, and Maddie—had decided to stay on campus the summer after their freshman year, she and Maddie had grown closer together. She felt if she could confide in anyone, it would be Maddie.

But she wasn't sure even Maddie would understand the restlessness she had been feeling lately. All her life, Stacy had been busy with an exhilarating schedule of worldly travel, glamorous parties, and important cultural events. Growing up in a wealthy family in Boston had given her a taste for excitement and constant variety. So staying on the campus of their small Georgia college for the summer was a pretty drastic shift into low gear.

At first it had worked out perfectly: The four girls had moved into one of the frat houses, and plunged right into their summer activities. And Stacy had eagerly looked forward to the amount of time she would be able to work on her ceramics projects—without annoying interruptions from classes and homework!

But somehow she had lost a lot of the energy she had started out with. Slumping forward, Stacy rested her chin on her palms, and stared blankly at her sculpture. *Face it, Stace. You're bored.*

There was something else that had been bothering her, too. Right before the end of the semester, her mother had announced, in her typical dramatic fashion, that she was getting divorced—for the fourth time. Sydney had insisted that Stacy spend the entire summer with her on Nantucket to "help get her through the rough times." And although Stacy had been sympathetic, she wondered now if her decision to stay in Georgia for the summer was really just a way to spite Sydney, a subtle form of revenge for all the times Syndey had let *her* down. There had been plenty of those.

"Maybe you just need a break," Maddie said gently.

Stacy met her friend's sympathetic gaze and let out a rueful chuckle. "You can say that again. Let's go get something to eat, okay?"

"Sure. But first I have to stop by the administration building to pick up my paycheck," Maddie said as she gathered up the armload of books that went everywhere with her. Both Maddie and Sam had summer jobs to make extra money for the coming school year.

Feeling better already, Stacy crossed the room to the sink and quickly washed the slimy red clay from her hands and forearms. With a quick glance for clay stains on the back of her khaki-colored sundress, she called over her shoulder, "No problem." Her eyes danced as she added, "Maybe I'll even make you pay."

"Fat chance. You've got clay on your forehead, by the way."

"Thanks." Stacy stripped off her apron and ran a wet paper towel across her face. "Am I even more beautiful now?" she teased.

Maddie rolled her eyes. "I'm not going to

answer that. Let's get out of here—I'm dying for some ice cream."

As they let themselves out of the Fine Arts Complex, a wave of intense heat stopped them in their tracks. The sun was blazing down from a cloudless, hazy sky, creating shimmering heat mirages along the campus paths. Only a handful of the students at Hawthorne for the summer were out in the blistering heat of midday.

"Yech." Stacy closed her eyes briefly, and tried to draw a breath of the humid air. "Do they have the air conditioning on in the administration building?" she muttered.

Maddie pulled her heavy dark hair into a ponytail and piled it up on the top of her head. "Yes. We could run over there, but we'd probably die of heat exhaustion before we even went ten feet."

"I don't care," Stacy said, squinting her eyes against the intense glare. The administration building wasn't far away, and most of the path was shaded by huge oak trees. "Let's just get over there. Come on." Grabbing Maddie's arm, she sprinted down the path.

Their breath was coming in short, harsh gasps by the time they reached the door to the building, and they dashed inside the cool, air-conditioned darkness with relief.

"Wow," Maddie sighed, leaning over to catch her breath with her hands on her knees. "Is it *hot*."

Nodding in silent agreement, Stacy wandered to a bench and sank onto it, fanning her throat with her hand. She looked up as Maddie passed her going down the hall to the bookkeeper's office.

"I'll be a few minutes. They always take forever to find checks."

Stacy nodded again. "Okay. I'll be here, don't worry." As Maddie disappeared around the corner, Stacy stretched her tanned, slender legs out in front of her and examined her red kidskin sandals critically. There was a dusty smudge of dried clay on one of her knees, which she rubbed off. Impatiently, she looked around her, wondering how long Maddie would take in the office. Her eyes strayed to a bulletin board, and she stood up to examine it, looking for a distraction.

The board was covered with notices about class scheduling changes for the coming year, apartments for rent, and campus jobs. Stacy read them without much interest. Then her gaze was caught by one small, handwritten note:

"Graduate student needs assistant in psychology lab to help finalize grant proposal. Clerical and organizational skills a must. A few hours a day, 3 to 4 weeks. Call Carter Cabbot, extension 4218."

For some reason, the name Carter Cabbot appealed to Stacy. It had such a distinctive air to it, she thought with a grin. Of course, she'd been surrounded by aristocratic-sounding Winthrops and Alexanders and Brandons all her life, and in her experience, most of them didn't live up to their high-class names. She smiled to herself, thinking about some of the more boring prep-school types she had met at debutante cotillions and charity balls over the years.

But her eyes wandered to the notice again. Two weeks before the end of summer vacation she was going up to Nantucket to visit Sydney. If the job was only three to four weeks, it would be over just before she needed to leave. And it was only a few hours every day. Maybe it would give her the kind of diversion she needed to revitalize her interest in ceramics, in Hawthorne— in *everything*.

"What's so fascinating about this bulletin board?" came Maddie's voice from behind her.

Stacy lifted one fair eyebrow with self-mockery. "Would you believe I'm thinking about applying for a campus job?"

"No! Not in a million years."

Chuckling, Stacy nodded. She reached in her bag for a pen. "Who knows? Maybe I'll actually *enjoy* earning money of my own."

"Some of us poor people find it pretty satisfying, let me tell you." Maddie folded her arms across her chest, and leaned against the wall. "What's the job?"

"Clerical help for some grad student," Stacy muttered, jotting down the name and phone number. She shrugged. "I probably won't actually call him, but I'm feeling virtuous."

"Why not? You should call, Stacy. It would be something to do."

Stacy chewed thoughtfully on her lower lip,

and looked at the slip of paper in her hand. Then she laughed. "Yeah. Why not?"

"It was a hundred today in Atlanta," announced Roni as she dropped onto a battered lawn chair on the frat house lawn after dinner.

Sam lifted her eyes from the book in her lap with a wry grin. "You actually sound proud of it."

"No, I'm just glad I'm not at home. I'd be roasting if I was," Roni drawled.

Stacy choked slightly on a swallow of Diet Coke. "I started roasting at eighty-five degrees, Roni. What does it take for you to overheat?"

With a nonchalant shrug, Roni crossed her legs. "A hundred and one degrees."

"I guess there's something to be said for growing up in the South then," Stacy quipped in a snobby tone. "Makes you immune to heat, does it?"

Roni darted her an evil look, and tossed her auburn curls back dramatically. "Yankee," she hissed. Then she grinned and turned to Sam. "Hey, isn't it getting kind of dark for reading?"

"I guess so." Sam answered. The cicadas buzzed gently in the twilight, and Sam heaved a weary sigh as she closed her book and leaned her head back against her chair. "Where's Maddie?"

Stacy slid down onto the grass to stretch out. It felt a few degrees cooler. "She said she was having dinner with Stu, but she should be back pretty soon." Rolling onto her back, she clasped her hands behind her neck and looked up at the darkening sky. A few stars were already coming out. In the distance some people called out to one another as they played Frisbee golf with a glow-in-the-dark disk. She wished her boyfriend, Pete Young, could be there with her, but he had been visiting out-of-town relatives for a week and wouldn't be back until the next day.

"Hi."

Stacy lifted her head. Maddie was walking up the path to the house with her boyfriend, Stu Peterson. "Hi, Stu."

He grinned and swung the shock of sandy hair that was always falling into his face out of his eyes. "How're you guys doing?" Turning to Maddie, he kissed her on the cheek. "See you tomorrow," he said softly.

All four girls watched as he strolled off into the gathering darkness. With a sigh, Maddie lowered herself onto the ground beside Stacy and crossed her legs. "Anything exciting going on here?"

"Not much," Roni chuckled.

Sam cleared her throat. "Actually . . ." She trailed off, looking into the distance.

Stacy frowned. "Yeah, Sam?"

"Well, I don't know if any of you noticed the sign in the Dining Commons, but we've got to decide about housing for next year. Soon."

"Oh. Well, I don't know," Stacy said, not very interested. She had assumed they would just get another suite like the one they had shared in Roger's House their freshman year. "It doesn't seem very urgent," she added, plucking idly at blades of grass at her side.

"Yeah, I know," Sam went on in a quiet voice, her face still hidden. "But Roni and I were talking, and, well, seeing as how you want to live at the sorority, and Maddie wants to stay on campus, Roni and I were thinking about getting an apartment somewhere."

Stacy's fingers stopped tearing at the grass. She had once mentioned living in Alpha Pi Alpha, the sorority she belonged to, but she hadn't been serious. Besides, there weren't usually many rooms available for sophomores in APA. So why did Sam just assume—? Or was it something else?

During the last few weeks of school, Sam and Roni had begun spending more and more time together, forming a mini-clique in their suite, while she and Maddie paired off. It hadn't really meant anything—it was usually just easier to do things in twos, rather than in fours. But maybe Roni and Sam were thinking they didn't want to live with her and Maddie anymore. As the thought took shape in Stacy's mind, her heart gave a painful lurch. Maybe this was their way of saying the group was finished.

"Okay," she said in an even tone, staring fixedly at the grass. Her head was spinning. "There are still some sophomore rooms at APA—I could try to get one of them."

There was a pause, and Stacy raised her eyes slowly. She thought Sam was looking at her, but in the darkness it was hard to tell. They had shared a bedroom for a year—and a lot more, too. Together, she and Sam had muddled through a hundred and one crises, from Sam's breakup with her hometown boyfriend, to Stacy's bout with anorexia, and dozens of other mini-tragedies in between. But suddenly, that was all over. Stacy looked away.

"What are you going to do, Maddie?" she asked as casually as she could.

The slender, dark-haired girl looked at her, and then at Roni and Sam. Of the four, Maddie was the newcomer. She had transferred to Hawthorne College at the beginning of the spring semester. At first, she had lived off campus with an aunt, but she had moved into their suite after spring break so that she could become more involved in campus activities. Obviously, she would not want to move off campus again after only half a term.

"I don't know," Maddie replied distantly. "I—I hadn't really thought about it. If I can get a single room in one of the dorms near the library, I guess that would be best."

So Maddie didn't want to live with her either, Stacy thought. Just like that, the foursome was broken apart, and nobody seemed to be very upset about it. It was hard to believe it could happen so quickly, and Stacy shook her head in confusion. She hesitated for a moment, trying to say something to slow things down, to get them to take a few moments to talk it over. But then the cool, objective side of her kept quiet. If they wanted to go separate ways, far be it from her to make a scene about it. That was definitely not Stacy Swanson's style.

She stood up and brushed bits of grass off her legs. "I guess I'll go to bed," she said as nonchalantly as she could.

No one said anything. The heavy summer air felt full of tension and the four girls exchanged apprehensive looks in the near darkness. The droning of the nighttime insects broke off abruptly, as though giving them all the chance to speak up. But no one said anything. Stacy paused for another long moment, and then turned on her heel and went into the house. Once inside, she brushed away a single tear.

As she climbed the stairs, she gazed blankly at the beer-stained, threadbare carpet, shaking her head. She should have said something, she told herself. She should have just told them she was hoping they would stay together. She even turned at the head of the stairs to go back down and tell them. But she stopped herself.

"I do have my pride," she told herself sternly. "If they don't want me, I'm not going to force myself on them. No Swanson has to *ask* for friends."

She headed down the corridor again, and paused, catching sight of the telephone. The slip of paper with the grad student's number on it was still in her purse. At least if she had a job it would keep her busy and out of the way of her roommates until it was time to go to Nantucket. She hurried to her room and came back with the number, and dialed the college switchboard.

"Extension 4218, please," she said quickly, pushing aside all her unhappy thoughts.

"That's an office number. There may not be anyone there at this hour."

Stacy closed her eyes with a tired sigh. Nothing was going right today. "Could you just try it, please?"

The operator gave an exasperated sigh, but made the connection. Stacy kept her eyes closed as the distant ringing sounded in her ear.

"Hello?"

She jumped, her eyes flying open at the sound of the smooth voice. "Oh—Oh, um. Is this—" She fumbled with the paper, trying to read her handwriting and realizing that she must sound like an idiot. "I'm sorry. Is this Carter Cabbot?"

"Yes."

"I saw your 'help wanted' ad for an assistant. Do you still need one?"

"Yes, I do. Are you a psychology student?"

A quick flush spread across Stacy's cheeks. How dumb of her not to think that that would be a requirement! "No," she admitted. "I'm not. Does it matter?"

Carter Cabbot laughed softly. "No, not at all. What's your name?"

"Stacy Swanson," she said, her confidence returning. "I can type, and I'm pretty organized, if that's what you're looking for."

"Mmm. More or less," came his voice, slightly teasing. "Tell me something about yourself. You sound like you're from Boston."

"That's right." She hesitated briefly before

adding, "Beacon Hill." She crossed her fingers, hoping she did the right thing by mentioning her socially prominent address.

"I have some family in that part of town," Carter Cabbot said, his voice warm and friendly. "Tell me, why aren't you up in Newport for the summer sailing?"

"Well, I'm not allowed to tell," she shot back quickly, her blue eyes dancing. "But the truth is, I get sea-sick."

There was a short pause on the other end of the line. Then Carter said, "I thought that was genetically impossible for someone from Beacon Hill. I'm amazed."

Stacy tried not to giggle. "Don't tell anyone, okay? I've got my reputation to think about."

"It's a deal," he assured her with a warm chuckle. "Listen, why don't you come by tomorrow and we can talk more, okay?"

Stacy felt a huge smile break out across her face. "Fine. What time?"

"Two o'clock? Room four hundred six in the Science Building."

"I'll be there."

"Good. I'm really looking forward to meeting you, Stacy."

As she hung up the phone, Stacy felt a strange rush of excitement. For some reason, she was really looking forward to meeting him, too.

Chapter 2

Stacy paused outside the door of room 406. She hadn't given herself a chance to think twice about the job since the night before, when she had spoken to Carter Cabbot. In retrospect, it seemed like a strange conversation, and she couldn't understand why it had left her so keyed up. After a morning at the ceramics studio, she had rushed back to Beta House to change her clothes, taking even more pains than usual with her appearance. And now, here she was, wondering if she had made a big mistake in coming here.

Stacy laughed at her seriousness. After all, just coming for an interview didn't mean that anything was cast in stone. If she didn't like the sound of the job, she didn't have to take it. So she had nothing to lose by meeting this guy. She raised her hand and rapped sharply on the door.

From inside came the sound of a chair scraping on the floor, and then footsteps approached. The door swung open.

"Hi. You must be Stacy."

Instantly, Stacy sized up the young man standing in front of her. She liked what she saw. He was tall and athletic-looking, but not brawny, with wavy dark hair and green eyes. He returned her searching look with amusement from behind horn-rimmed glasses. Sensuous lips curled up into a lopsided grin, revealing a dimple in his left cheek. In that split second Stacy decided he was very attractive, and just as quickly, reminded herself that it didn't make any difference what he looked like. After all, she wasn't looking for romance—just a job, a diversion.

Nodding agreement, Stacy put out her hand, which he shook warmly. "I'm Stacy Swanson. Glad to meet you."

"Well, come on in," he said. He stepped aside and ushered her in with a polite gesture. "Take a seat, Stacy." He crossed the tiny, cluttered office to his desk, and sat down, casually crossing his legs. Stacy noticed he wore khakis and Italian loafers with no socks, the standard dress code of the laid-back preppy. Something told her she knew a lot about him already. She knew instinctively that they came from the same world.

For a long moment, the two regarded one another silently. Stacy felt she was being appraised in the same way she had looked at him, but she also knew she was passing the test. She felt pleased, but nervous, and she had to tell herself not to be silly. Just because a handsome man looked at her didn't mean she had to act like a naive school girl. She had a boyfriend, anyway.

His smile widened and he leaned forward on his elbows, taking off his glasses.

"Tell me something about yourself," he said, holding her gaze steadily. "I already know you're not a sailor, and you're not a psychology major. What is your major, by the way?"

She grinned wryly. "I'm an art major—studio and art history, I guess. I haven't declared it yet, but I'm pretty sure that's what it will be."

"You haven't declared your major yet?" he repeated with a puzzled frown. "Isn't it a little late for that? You're a senior, aren't you?"

Rolling her eyes, Stacy shook her head. She tried not to let him see how pleased she was by the compliment. "No—this past year was my freshman year. Three more to go, I'm afraid."

"I don't believe it," Carter said.

She shrugged. "Believe it."

Carter leaned back in his chair and crossed his arms across his chest. "Okay," he said, his vivid green eyes alight with admiration. "I believe you. So, what's your field in art history? No, wait! Let me guess. The French Impressionists, right? Degas, Monet, Renoir."

"That's right," Stacy replied with surprise. "How did you know?"

He stared intently into her eyes again. "I just knew, that's all."

Under his steady gaze, Stacy was surprised to feel her cheeks growing warm. The man definitely has charm, she told herself with a silent salute of admiration. Stacy wryly observed he was just the type of guy her mother went for. She cleared her throat.

"Well, do you want me to take a—a typing test or anything?"

He laughed richly, running one hand through his dark hair. "That won't be necessary. Why don't I just tell you about this project so you know what you're getting yourself into."

Leaning forward again on his elbows, Carter became instantly serious. Stacy listened, mesmerized.

"What I'm working on has the potential to rock the world of psychology," he explained in an earnest voice, his green eyes kindling with an inner fire. "Do you know anything about behaviorism, Stacy?"

She shook her head. "Sorry."

"Well, never mind. You will soon," he continued. "The work I'm doing will disprove behaviorism once and for all, but I need to get some research money to complete the experiments. That's where this grant comes in. The National Science Foundation is making some money available to Hawthorne College, and I need it. So my presentation has to be impressive—it has to hit them right between the eyes. I *need* that money, Stacy," he repeated emphatically, staring deeply into her eyes.

She nodded automatically, her eyes locked on his.

The electric intensity in the air vanished as Carter's face broke into a disarming smile. "We scientists can get pretty passionate about our work," he said in a quieter tone. "You'll find that out pretty soon."

For a moment, Stacy was too hypnotized to catch the significance of his words. She shook her head to clear the cobwebs. "You mean—I've got the job?"

"If you want it."

Stacy knew she wanted it. The charismatic Carter Cabbot promised to add excitement to the rest of her summer—intellectual excitement, she corrected herself hastily. "Yes," she heard herself say, as if she was in a trance. "I want the job."

"Good. I'm glad, Stacy. I know I'll enjoy working with you. How about having dinner with me tonight? I could tell you more about the project," he added casually. "We could share a bottle of Cabernet Sauvignon. Part business, part pleasure."

Stacy lowered her eyes, shocked at the jump her heart had made at his invitation. But she had already made plans: she had a dinner date with Pete. She shook her head firmly.

"Sorry. I'm having dinner with my boyfriend." She said the last word quietly, keeping her eyes lowered to her lap.

"Oh. I see."

Was it her imagination, or was there a trace of disappointment in his voice? Stacy was used to turning down men's invitations—but for once, she regretted doing it. And that was what worried her: What did it mean? She told herself to be sensible, that she was interested in hearing more about the work she would be doing for him. And besides, there was nothing wrong in admitting that she might enjoy his company, after all. He was interesting, intelligent, and they seemed to have a lot in common. That was a rare occurrence at Hawthorne.

"Well," she said brightly, rising to her feet. "I guess I should be going. When do you want me to start?"

Carter stood up, too. "First thing tomorrow?"

"Fine. Nine o'clock?"

He held out his hand, and she took it. The warmth of his handshake ran up her arm, and she broke eye contact quickly and turned away. As she reached for the door, his voice made her look back.

"See you tomorrow at nine, Stacy."

Their eyes locked again, and then Stacy hurried out the door.

As Stacy let her Mercedes roll to a stop in front of the Youngs' rambling Victorian house, the front door opened and a mob of young kids tumbled out, followed more slowly and sedately by their big brother, Pete.

"Stacy! Stacy!" With their excited voices they

sounded like little birds as the seven-year-old twins and their ten-year-old sister called to her from the front steps. Around the door peeped Pete's teen-aged sisters, Alice and Margaret. "Bye, Pete! Bye, Stacy! Bye-bye!" One of the family dogs joined in with the general howling, and inside the house, the baby let out an eager screech.

Stacy grinned as Pete climbed into the front seat, and their eyes met. "Hi," she said with a laugh.

"Hi yourself," he murmured. He touched her cheek and leaned toward her to kiss her. The chorus of Pete's little brothers and sisters rose to a crescendo of ecstatic shrieks, and Stacy burst out laughing. As she put the car into reverse she shook her head. "Your family is amazing, Pete," she chuckled, her eyes darting to the rear view mirror while she slowly backed down the driveway, carefully avoiding all of the miscellaneous bikes and wagons.

"What can I say? They like you," Pete replied warmly. His voice was husky as he added, "So do I."

Stacy felt a lump in her throat. "I really missed you, Pete. I'm glad you're back."

There was an expectant silence as Stacy drove across town and into the parking lot of the Dixie Diner. She cut the engine and sat staring ahead of her, feeling strangely upset. For the past twenty-four hours, her emotions had been in a tailspin: first from finding out her roommates didn't want to live with her, and then from meeting the dynamic Carter Cabbot. She forced herself to put Carter out of her mind.

"What's wrong, Stace? What is it?" Pete asked.

She looked at Pete's comforting, familiar face—the strong jawline, warm blue-green eyes and touseled red hair. Her shoulders sagged a little with weariness. Without a word, Pete reached over to Stacy and put his arms around her. All through the months of their relationship, Pete had had an uncanny knack for knowing when something was wrong, and he usually didn't push her to talk, something she was always grateful for. Stacy had always been a very private person, concealing her feelings behind a fragile mask of beauty and expensive clothes. Pete was one of the few people who knew how imperfect her glamorous life had been. So he just let her know he was there if and when she felt like letting go.

"Sam and Roni are getting an apartment together," she said at last in a low voice. She rubbed her cheek against his warm, strong shoulder. "They didn't even ask me or Maddie if we wanted to live with them."

Pete pulled back a bit to look into her face. "You're kidding!"

Miserable, she shook her head, and then shrugged her shoulders in resignation. "I don't even know what to think about it. I mean, one minute we were all getting along great, and then pow—out of the blue, Sam says since I'm obviously moving into APA, they're getting an apartment together. And that's that."

"Sounds like . . . I don't know." Pete frowned, chewing his lower lip thoughtfully. "Sounds like they're trying to squeeze you out, and they used the sorority as an excuse or something," he suggested in a troubled voice. "But you know, it really doesn't sound like them. Especially Sam."

"I know," she agreed sadly. "I just couldn't believe it."

"Well, what about Maddie? What's she going to do?"

Stacy rolled her eyes. "Well as soon as Roni and Sam said *they* were getting an apartment, I said I guess I would live at APA—I didn't know what else to say! And then Maddie jumped right in and said she was going to live in one of the dorms near the library."

"But you don't *have* to live at APA, do you? I mean, you could share a suite with Maddie, right?"

"Yeah," Stacy admitted reluctantly. "But it didn't sound like she was very interested in it. She didn't suggest it or anything." She couldn't even admit to Pete how hurt she was, nor could she bring herself to suggest something different to her roommates now that everything seemed to be so settled.

Pete gave her a reassuring hug. "Listen, let's just go have a nice, relaxing meal and forget about it for a while, okay? I know things will work out, Stacy. Don't worry about it."

"That's easy for you to say," she muttered as

she shut her door and locked it. Hand in hand they strolled into the Dixie Diner, a favorite greasy-spoon hangout for kids at Hawthorne College.

As they slid into the booth, Pete reached for her hand again across the table, and gave her a warm smile. "So, what did I miss while I was away? Any interesting gossip? Any new news?"

Stacy smiled in response. She hesitated to tell him about her job with Carter Cabbot. All her instincts told her to keep it out of the conversation, but her common sense told her there was nothing to hide. Gently she released her fingers from his clasp, and toyed idly with her fork.

"I got a job as an assistant in the psych lab," she said casually. "I'll be helping a grad student get a proposal ready for some kind of grant."

Pete opened the plastic-covered menu and ran his eyes down it quickly. "Sounds interesting," he said absentmindedly. "What kind of research is he or she doing?"

"Oh, it's a he. I don't know exactly what it is—I don't even care, it's just something to do," Stacy replied in a breezy tone. For some reason she couldn't pin down, she didn't want to fill Pete in any more than necessary. "So, what are you having?"

He shrugged. "A burger. How about you?"

"Hmm . . ." Looking without enthusiasm at the Diner's plain old offerings, she felt a sudden rush of exasperation. "I could really go for some calimari," she said glumly.

"Calimari? What's that? Pete never felt self-conscious admitting he didn't know something, a trait that Stacy admired. For her, it was important at least to *seem* to know everything, and sometimes it put her in awkward situations.

"Squid," she informed him.

He chuckled. "Not for me, thanks."

"Ever tried it?"

"No, and I don't intend to."

Stacy gritted her teeth, fighting a growing sense of impatience. Stacy appreciated Pete's candor and the simplicity with which he approached life, but sometimes she wished he was a little more adventurous.

"It wouldn't hurt you to try something new," she insisted, keeping her eyes fixed on the menu.

"Well they don't seem to be serving cali-whatever tonight so it looks like I'm in luck," Pete said with another light chuckle. "Come on, what'll you have that's *on* the menu?"

She sighed heavily and pushed the menu away as a waitress approached. "Tuna salad plate, rye crisps and a large Diet Coke. With lots of ice, please."

"And I'll have a cheeseburger special deluxe plate," Pete added, giving the waitress a friendly smile. "Make it medium-well done, and I'll have a vanilla malted with that, please."

Stacy glanced at her boyfriend through her lashes. Many times she had wondered how he would handle himself at one of her father's numerous political gatherings—among ambassadors and congressmen, important journalists and members of the jet set. She had mingled with an elite group all her life, and attending elegant parties was second nature to her. But if she brought Pete to a sophisticated dinner party, would he still want a plain old hamburger?

As soon as that thought flashed into her mind, she scolded herself for reverting to her old snobbish ways. Pete was Pete, and she loved him. What difference did it really make if he didn't know a lobster fork from a fruit knife, a champagne flute from a brandy snifter? Those were all such meaningless ways to judge character. Both of her parents had all the social graces, and Pete was a nicer, more polite person than both of them.

Thinking of her mother reminded her of her upcoming trip. "So I'm all set for Nantucket," she said nervously. "I thought I'd stop by Boston and see the new Surrealists' exhibition at the Museum of Fine Arts before I head back."

Pete nodded politely, but his blank expression told her he wasn't very interested in the Surrealists. She took a long drink of her Diet Coke. She had always known what Pete was like. It just never bothered her before now.

Unfortunately, she had to admit that it did bother her—more than just a little.

Chapter 3

"Stacy? Is that you?" Sam's voice called out from the adjoining room as Stacy let herself into their suite at the fraternity.

She tossed her alligator-skin handbag toward a chair, and watched dejectedly as it missed by several inches and skidded across the floor. "Yeah."

Sam came into the room dressed in nylon running shorts and a tank top. "Where've you been?" she asked, dragging a brush through her shoulder-length hair. "We missed you at dinner."

"Out with Pete." Dropping gracefully into a chair, Stacy let her chin sink into her chest and she stared glumly at the floor. For the first time, "Out with Pete" had not been the same thing as "Out having fun." She pulled herself together with an effort and managed a smile. "So what did I miss at dinner?"

"Oh." Sam shrugged slightly, and turned her face away. "We were—you know. Talking about our living arrangements for next year," she said quietly.

Stacy stared hard at the back of Sam's head, her heart turning over painfully. Obviously, Sam wanted some reassurance that Stacy was going ahead with plans to move on her own. Prickling with a mixture of hurt and anger, Stacy pushed herself up and headed for the bedroom.

"I'm going over to APA tomorrow," she announced in a cool voice as she paused in the doorway. "There's an announcement about a room lottery for sophomores posted in the dining room."

There was no response from Sam, and Stacy glanced over her shoulder. Sam's face was still averted, but Stacy could see that her friend's cheek were tinged with a deep blush over her tan.

She's probably embarrassed about being so rude, Stacy told herself cynically. *And she should be.*

"Well," Sam continued, "I guess Roni and I will start apartment hunting tomorrow, then."

Swallowing painfully, Stacy nodded. She pushed open the bedroom door and slipped inside, then leaned back against the door and closed her eyes. It was definite, then, and there was no turning back. For a moment, she felt like she was reliving the awful weeks before Thanksgiving when she had alienated her friends, blown her chances to win a race for sorority pledge representative, and discovered that neither of her parents wanted to see her for the holidays. She had thought then that things could never be that bad again.

"Well," she muttered grimly. "Looks like I was wrong."

For an instant, she had a vision of herself lying on the beach in Nantucket. All she wanted was to let the sun shine strongly on her and melt away her problems, and to let the chilly Atlantic wash away her doubts and anxieties. But she knew she couldn't go there yet.

From the other side of the closed door came the sound of knocking and Sam's footsteps followed by a low murmur of voices. Then there was a hesitant knock on the door Stacy was leaning against.

"Stacy? There's a call for you on the phone in the hall—it's your mother."

Stifling a groan, Stacy rubbed one hand across her tired eyes. The thought of talking to Sydney was depressing and she searched her mind frantically for some way to get out of it. But she knew perfectly well that when Sydney was on the warpath, it only made things worse to stall her.

"I'll be right there!" she called. Taking a deep breath, she went back into the outer room and then out into the corridor.

"Hi, Sydney."

"Stacy, why in God's good name do you have to stay in that dismal Hayseed Springs *all* summer?" Her mother's voice came crackling over the telephone line. Stacy could just picture her posed artistically in an expensive imitation 'rustic' lounge chair on the beach house deck, dragging heavily on a cigarette while the waves crashed on the beach. Sydney had a definite flair for setting a scene—and for making one.

"*Hawthorne* Springs, Sydney. And I told you—"

"I know, I know, darling. It's important to your personal growth to be there—you told me *ad nauseum*. But Stacy honey, what about *my* personal growth? This divorce is stunting me for life. That illiterate, vulgar boor—"

"David?" Stacy broke in with heavy sarcasm. Her mother's fourth husband had beaten all the records: they were married in November, and split up in June. And her mother had insisted she loved David the most.

"Yes, *David*. Don't be snide, darling. It's in such poor taste at your age."

Stacy drew in a deep breath to steady her nerves. Now she knew why she didn't want to spend any more time than absolutely necessary with Sydney that summer. She might be restless in Hawthorne Springs, but it was one hundred per cent better than being angry in Nantucket. So much for the sun and the ocean.

"I just can't believe he has the *gall*, that he

would stoop so *low* as to insist on my settling half the art gallery on him," Sydney fumed. "The depth to which that man has sunk is truly unfathomable."

With an impatient grimace, Stacy held the phone away from her ear so her mother's stream of elegantly phrased abuse against David dissolved into a distant, meaningless babble. Her eyes focused on a phone number scribbled on the wall as she tried to take an objective look at her life. Her mother was bent on pulling everyone and everything around her into her own anger and depression; her roommates didn't seem to care too much about her anymore; she felt strangely dissatisfied with Pete; and her father was off in Alaska with his twenty-year-old girlfriend, getting 'back to nature.'

My life is unbelievable, Stacy decided with calm detachment. *It's too unbelievable even for a soap opera.*

"Stacy? Are you there?"

Startled, she brought the receiver back to her ear again and hastily soothed her mother. "Yes, Sydney. I feel really bad about it, but I know you can pull through. I've got a ton of stuff I have to take care of down here, but I'll be coming up real soon, okay?"

Sydney sniffed cynically. "You're even beginning to sound like a Southerner." Stacy held her breath, wishing the conversation would end. "Okay, darling. Come as soon as you can. And listen—it's not too late for you to think about taking next semester off, you know. You could even work at the gallery."

"We'll talk about that when I'm there," Stacy said firmly. "I really have to go now, Sydney. Someone else needs to use the phone. Bye."

She dropped the receiver into its cradle before her mother could say anything else. She leaned her head back against the wall. It seemed like she didn't have enough energy to stand up at all lately. She didn't know if it was the heat and humidity that was sapping her strength, or if she was just sinking into a depression. But talking to Sydney definitely emphasized how awful her situation had become.

Briefly she toyed with the idea of taking a semester off and staying at home. But that wouldn't really solve anything. One lesson she had learned in her eating disorders group was that you couldn't make your problems go away—by dieting, by running away, or by covering them up. No, she had to stay at Hawthorne.

The one thing she could be grateful for was her new job, she reasoned. That gave her a spark of hope. At least she could throw herself into that. And if she was lucky, she'd be able to get her mind off other things for a while. More and more, Carter Cabbot and his project looked like they might turn out to be the best part of an otherwise horrible summer.

Stacy stood in front of the mirror, holding a light pink cotton dress up against her lacy camisole.

Then she puckered her mouth in distaste and threw the dress over her shoulder. It was too feminine-looking to wear to work.

Returning to the closet, she pulled a white linen camp shirt and a slim blue skirt off the hangers and held them up for examination. With her flat, white, gladiator-style sandals, they would project just the right image: cool and business-like, but stylish. She stepped quickly into the skirt and buttoned it around her narrow waist.

As she slipped her arms into the crisp linen blouse, Roni appeared in the doorway behind her, leaning against the frame. Their eyes met in the mirror, and Roni's dark auburn eyebrows rose a fraction while Stacy fingered the buttons into place.

"Looks like someone wants to impress the new boss," Roni said after a few moments, an impish grin on her face. "What a good girl."

Stacy shrugged carelessly, and concentrated on putting in a pair of lapis lazuli earrings. "Nothing wrong with that, I hope?"

"Nah. Makes me wonder what the boss looks like, though." Roni's smile grew wider.

In one swift movement, Stacy reached for a fuzzy stuffed rabbit and tossed it at Roni's head. Roni let out yelp and ducked quickly.

"You and your dirty mind," Stacy said with mock severity as she breezed past Roni through the doorway.

Roni giggled, and caught Stacy in the back

with the same poor bunny. For a moment, Stacy
could almost believe things were the way they
always had been, with all the easy joking and
friendly teasing. But with a stab of nostalgia, she
remembered that it was all about to end in a few
weeks. Squaring her shoulders, Stacy left the
suite without a backward glance. She was not
going to let herself think about Roni.

But as she let herself out the front door and
trotted down the steps, her thoughts wandered
back to Roni's not-so-subtle hint. There was
nothing wrong with looking nice, though—Stacy
could afford an impressive wardrobe and she
enjoyed showing it off. And if lately she had
been getting a little sloppy, it was definitely time
to start shaping up again. Her new job simply
provided a good excuse.

The office door was standing wide open when
she arrived. She looked in and a wave of
nervousness and excitement rippled through
her.

Carter, seated at his desk with a pile of papers,
looked up with a small smile and beckoned to
her. "Stacy! Come on in. Let's get started. We've
got a lot to do."

"Oh, sure," she replied woodenly. His dramatic shift from flirtatiousness to no-nonsense took
her by surprise, and she realized she had been
looking forward to a repeat of their first meeting. Hastily she stowed her shoulder bag on a
bookshelf, and followed Carter to the typewriter.

"Now, my handwriting has never won any

prizes," he said, flashing her another quick smile as he scooped up a stack of notes. "Just do your best with these—I'm not looking for a finished manuscript, just a clean copy I can work on. Triple space, and leave big margins."

Stacy nodded automatically as she pulled out the chair and put the pile of notes beside her. Just as she was about to speak, Carter moved away and busied himself at his desk. With an inward, self-mocking smile, Stacy rolled a sheet of paper into the typewriter. Apparently the man was not swept away by either her charm or her appearance, she decided wryly.

Well, that's just fine, she thought as she squinted at his notes, feeling vaguely let down. *I'm here to work, so I'll work.*

The noisy clacking of typewriter keys filled the small office, interrupted by long pauses as Stacy pored over Carter's illegible handwriting. Several times she had to ask Carter to decipher something for her, which he did with a preoccupied air. She half-expected him to strike up a conversation each time she interrupted him, but he always went right back to work.

Resigning herself to 'strictly business,' Stacy labored away with the notes for Carter's proposal. For the most part, she didn't follow the line of argument he was setting out, and the technical psychology terms meant nothing to her. But she found herself wishing she understood enough to ask intelligent questions.

Finally she cleared her throat. "Carter?"

"Yes?" He turned to her, a questioning lift to his eyebrows. The look of intense absorption on his face made him more serious and more attractive at the same time. "Another illegible word?"

She grinned. "No, I just wondered—I know I sound impossibly stupid, but what exactly *is* behaviorism?"

"Ah. Well," he answered slowly. He took off his glasses and dangled them from two fingers. He seemed to be thinking hard about how to explain. "Behaviorism is a school of psychology which is concerned with responses to environmental stimuli—the once burned, twice shy syndrome."

Seeing her puzzled look, he grinned. "Basically, it adheres to the notion that all behavior is based on reward and punishment. Behaviorists put rats in mazes and give them cheese when they reach the end. Or a jolt of electricity if they mess up." He sneered slightly. "That's how it goes in a high school experiment, anyway."

"But I—" Stacy bit her lower lip. She hated to seem so ignorant. "I'm not sure why you disagree."

"Well, look. Say you wanted to get tickets to hear Vladimir Horowitz play with the Boston Symphony." He broke off as Stacy grinned. "And if they were sold out, does that mean you would never try again?"

"Actually . . ." Stacy's lips twitched and she

lowered her eyes. "I'd probably call the governor—he usually has tickets to spare."

There was a short silence. Stacy looked up to find Carter gazing at her with a mixture of admiration and amusement.

"Suppose he could get me in to see the American Ballet Theatre when they tour next fall?" he asked.

Stifling a giggle, Stacy nodded. "I can ask." Then she laughed out loud. "He got me in last fall," she admitted with a grin.

Carter laughed with her, his eyes glowing. "You saw them last fall—in Boston?" She nodded. "I was there, too."

"You're kidding!" Stacy exclaimed.

He shook his head solemnly, and turned in his chair to face her directly. "Would I lie to you, Stacy?" he said in a meaningful tone. "After the show I ate at the restaurant on top of the Prudential Center."

With a sigh, Stacy propped her elbows on the typewriter and rested her chin in her hands. "That's one of my favorite places in Boston. You can see just about the whole city."

They sat smiling at one another for what seemed to Stacy like an eternity; and her heart didn't seem to beat at all during that time.

Carter cleared his throat. "Getting back to my point," he said softly. "I, for one, try and try until I get what I want. I don't let setbacks get in my way."

There was no mistaking his message, and

Stacy turned away quickly and let out a long breath.

The phone rang shrilly, breaking the electric charge between them. Frowning, Carter picked it up and Stacy bent over the pages of notes again. There was no question in her mind that Carter Cabbot was stimulating company—especially in comparison with the general atmosphere of the Hawthorne campus in the summertime.

Her fingers fumbled over the keys as she thought how nice it was to meet someone like Carter, someone she had so much in common with right there in Hawthorne Springs. Then she swallowed hard. *Nice* wasn't the word, she admitted with difficulty. That was something the Beacon Hill matrons might say. Fantastic was closer to the truth.

Chapter 4

Stacy floated to the Dining Commons in a daze, oblivious to the sights and sounds around her. She went through the motions of getting her lunch on automatic pilot, pushing her tray along and mechanically reaching for a fork, knife, spoon, napkin. Then she came to a standstill, gazing blankly at the man behind the counter.

"Beef stew or grilled cheese sandwich?" he prompted wearily. The man was glowing from the kitchen heat, and Stacy looked at the steaming dishes with a shudder.

"I'll just get salad bar," she muttered quickly, reaching for a glass of iced tea. She hurried out into the Dining Commons, which was less than half-filled with summer students.

I must be in bad shape, she realized as she

piled lettuce and green peppers and tomato slices on her plate at the big salad bar in the middle of the room. *I'm spacing out like a teenager.*

"Well, well, well. If it isn't the lab assistant of the year," came Roni's teasing voice over her shoulder.

Stacy turned, the salad tongs poised. Arching one eyebrow, Stacy dropped a broccoli spear on her plate. "In the flesh," she announced.

Roni's green eyes danced with curiosity, and she nodded toward the window. "Come on. We're sitting over there. And we demand to hear the full story."

Resisting a wild impulse to giggle, Stacy drizzled oil and vinegar over her salad and then followed her roommate. Sam and Maddie were seated at a round table for four.

"Here she is," Roni announced airily as she manuevered around the tables ahead of Stacy. "She's going to tell us what it's like to be gainfully employed by a mysterious, but no doubt gorgeous, grad student."

Stacy set down her tray and pulled out a chair, shaking her head. "I haven't the foggiest idea why you leap to that conclusion, Veronica." But she could feel herself grinning, and she caught the questioning looks in her friends' eyes.

Roni dropped into her chair. "Well? Is he or isn't he?"

After she took a sip of iced tea, Stacy looked at the ice cubes tinkling in her glass. Finally she raised her eyes with an unconcerned smile. "Is or isn't he what?" she asked politely.

"Come on, Swanson," Roni warned, pointing a fork at her. "We want all the gory details."

Stacy smiled serenely. "Well then, he is, as a matter of fact."

"Mysterious or gorgeous?" Maddie prompted eagerly.

"Gorgeous. But who cares? The work I'm doing is really interesting," Stacy continued quickly as her enthusiasm bubbled over. She could still see Carter's face, transformed by his dedication to his work. "He explained all about his research and it's fascinating. It's pretty advanced stuff, I guess. I mean, I can barely understand it at all."

"Well, what did you do all morning with this gorgeous, fascinating guy?" Sam asked with a grin as she bit into her grilled cheese.

"Well, mostly typing—"

"*Typing*?" Roni gasped. She smacked her forehead with one open palm in a typically melodramatic gesture. "Stacy, you don't even type your *own* papers. What made you think you wanted to do it for someone else?"

"Maybe it has something to do with the level of gorgeousness we're talking about," Maddie suggested in a knowing tone as she tore a brownie in two. She looked up with an innocent expression on her heart shaped face. "Isn't that what they call fringe benefits?"

Roni narrowed her eyes suspiciously. "Sure is.

I can see it all now: Stacy falls madly in love with her boss, and becomes his very own personal secretary—for life."

"Don't be ridiculous," Stacy said with a breathless laugh. Carter's words came back to her clearly, making her heart speed up. She poked busily at her salad as she insisted, "That's the stupidest thing I've ever heard, Roni. You know, it's impossible to talk to a man around here without it being cause for major scandal."

"We'll see about the scandal part," Roni teased. She rested her chin in her hands and peered intently into Stacy's eyes. "I see into your soul," she intoned in an eerie gypsy voice. "Anastasia Vaughn Swanson! I can read your secret thoughts. There is a man in there; is it Pete Young, or someone else?"

Feeling slightly shaken, Stacy forced herself to smile. As a matter of fact, she hadn't given Pete too much thought lately. She began to worry that the conversation might be heading for dangerous territory.

"The only thing in my secret thoughts right now is revenge against the person who thought of serving *that* in July," she retorted, pointing at Roni's beef stew with her fork. "It takes a sick mind to come up with something like that on a ninety-degree day."

Roni grinned and stuffed a heaping forkful of stew into her mouth. "Mmmm. Delicious," she mumbled.

"I think there's more to this research project

than meets the eye," Sam continued. She tapped her chin thoughtfully with one finger and pursed her lips. "I think Stacy is secretly planning to run away with this guy."

"That's right," cut in Maddie, holding out her hand dramatically as she closed her eyes. "She risked it all for the man she loved!"

"Their passion knew no bounds," added Roni, picking up their romance novel style. With her hands clasped to her heart she moaned, "Which one would she choose—the loyal, good-hearted man who loved her truly, or the dangerous but irresistible scoundrel who stole her heart? Stay tuned, dear reader—"

"For the best—and hottest—is yet to come," Sam finished. She giggled into her napkin.

Roni scooted her chair up next to Stacy's and put her face inches away. "Have we got the story more or less accurate, Miss Swanson, or would you like to fill us in on all the details?"

"Oh, cut it out!" Stacy snapped. The others looked surprised, and Stacy prayed she wasn't blushing. "Can't we talk about something more interesting than my non-existent love affair?" she went on in a bored tone. "Besides I'm not one of those people who likes to think or talk about my job when I'm not there. So much for my dedication," she quipped.

"Well," Roni huffed. She dug into her beef stew again, but she looked like she still had something to say.

Silence descended on the group, and the

noise of everyone else's conversations in the Dining Commons seemed more noticable. Stacy felt foolish for letting herself get so upset by their teasing, but she didn't feel like talking about Carter. Maybe they would just let the subject drop.

"Roni had a great idea," Sam announced uneasily as she pushed away her plate. "Let's have some kind of special party or celebration on our last night together—just before you leave for Nantucket, Stace. We could go to a fancy restaurant or something, just the four of us."

Maddie sent Stacy a sharp look before she nodded. "Sounds like a good idea—maybe we could go to L'Auberge. I've heard it's really special. What do you think, Stacy?"

She nodded slowly. Their last night together didn't sound like cause for celebration to her, but she didn't want to let them know how hurt she was feeling about their plans for next year. "Sure. That sounds good to me."

"Great. It's all settled, then," Roni said enthusiastically. "And let's make it a night to remember."

Stacy climbed the front steps of the elegant white house that was home to Alpha Pi Alpha sorority and paused in the shade of the wide verandah. APA was the most popular and influential sorority on campus, and it was considered quite a feat to pledge and be accepted.

There had been a time when Stacy thought living at APA would be the highlight of her years at Hawthorne. Now she wasn't so sure.

Lost in thought, she sank slowly into a white wicker chair and stared out across the porch railing. She had so many good memories of the APA house: parties, meetings, pledge week jitters. But she had even more good memories of living in Rogers House. And suddenly she knew she couldn't let it end without saying something.

"I'll just tell them," she said out loud as a bird landed on the railing and looked at her brightly. The bird bobbed its head, and Stacy laughed. "You think that's a good idea, huh? So do I."

With a new sense of urgency, she hurried down the steps and headed for Beta House. Just as she arrived, Roni and Sam stepped out of the front door.

"Hi," Stacy gasped, looking up the steps at them. She paused to catch her breath while her friends watched her expectantly.

"Listen," she began earnestly, one hand clutching the banister for support. "I was just over at APA—"

"Did you sign up for the room lottery?" Sam interrupted, an anxious look in her brown eyes.

Stacy shut her mouth with a snap. She felt like she had just been slapped in the face. Obviously, Sam and Roni were determined to exclude her and Maddie. And there was no way she was going to humiliate herself now.

"No—but I will, don't worry," she said flippantly. She tossed her head back. "Have you two found your dream apartment yet?"

Roni and Sam exchanged a look. "No," Roni admitted. "We were just going to look at some places now," she said quietly.

"Oh." Stacy nodded and leaned back against the banister. "Don't jump at the first thing you see," she suggested, casually crossing her ankles and trying to look unconcerned. "And don't let any landlords take you for a ride. Make sure everything is spelled out in a lease."

Sam nodded. "We won't." She swallowed hard, and glanced furtively at Roni. "Would you, um, do you want to come with us?"

For a moment, Stacy kept a careless smile plastered on her face while her insides twisted into a tight knot. *How can they rub it in like this?* she screamed silently. Then she drew a deep breath and managed a small shrug. "No, thanks—I have a million things to do this afternoon."

"Well, if you're sure."

Stacy met Roni's level gaze. "Sure, I'm sure. See you later."

Turning swiftly, Stacy headed back the way she had come. Her pace quickened as she ducked out of sight behind a huge, spreading tulip tree, and she started to race for the APA house, fighting the urge to cry.

Holly Dieter was sitting on the porch when Stacy ran up the steps, and raised her hand in a wave. Stacy stopped and turned to look at her.

"Hi, Holly."

Holly smiled. "Hi, Stacy. Hot, isn't it?"

"Yeah, I guess so," Stacy said. She frowned at the door. "Listen, are there still some rooms available in the house next year for sophomores"

"I think so, but the draw isn't until next week. You don't really have to sign up until then, you know."

Stacy gritted her teeth. "Well, I'm here now, so I might as well," she said. She hoped Holly couldn't tell how upset she was.

"Well sure, why not." Holly stretched lazily, and ruffled her hair with one hand. "But I didn't know you wanted to move into the house. I thought you and your roommates really got along great. Why aren't you guys living together again?"

With one hand on the doorknob, Stacy stared at the porch floor, staring at the tiny lines in the gray paint. What would Holly think if she told her the truth? Popular Stacy Swanson, APA pledge representative and considered one of the most glamorous members of the sorority, wasn't even asked to live with her old roommates.

"Things change," she said. She looked up and met Holly's enquiring glance. "So where do I sign up?"

The wad of clay made a thud as it landed on the table and Stacy began pounding out the air bubbles. With one muddy hand she peeled it up and wedged it again, her eyes narrowed with concentration. Mechanically she picked it up again and slammed it down onto the table.

"Sounds like you're trying to kill that piece of clay."

Stacy whirled around in surprise and met Pete's eyes. He grinned and looked pointedly at the flattened lump of clay.

"Oh, it just needs a good wedging, that's all," she muttered as she turned back to the workbench again. Pete's footsteps sounded on the cool tile floor as he came up behind her and wrapped his arms around her waist. She tried to worm her way out of his grasp.

"What's wrong?" he asked, his blue eyes puzzled.

Stacy dropped her gaze, annoyed with herself for being so mean to Pete. But she also felt a strange, purposeless anger, and she scowled at the clay on her table. "You'll get filthy, that's all," she said. "I'm covered with clay."

Pete laughed as he hitched himself up onto a stool. "Never bothered me when I was cleaning here," he drawled in his smooth Southern voice. They had met in the ceramics studio when Pete was doing some janitorial work for his campus job. "Besides, I was born with red Georgia clay under my fingernails, remember?"

Stacy didn't say anything. She scraped up the wedged clay again and walked over to an electric potter's wheel. Climbing onto the seat, she planted the lump of clay on the center of the wheel and switched it on with her foot. She dipped her hands in a bucket of water and leaned forward with her arms supported on her knees. She watched the clay spin around and around. Glancing at Pete from the corner of her eye, Stacy managed a weak smile. Then she placed her wet hands on either side of the spinning clay and began pressing it firmly.

"Want to tell me what's wrong?" Pete asked.

She made a slight, impatient gesture with her shoulders. "It's nothing, Pete," she muttered, keeping her eyes fixed on the clay while she pressed her thumbs down into the middle. She didn't want to meet his steady gaze: If he did look into her eyes, what would he see? She didn't even know herself.

He sighed, and pushed himself off the stool. "Okay."

Stacy glanced at him again, but her eyes darted back to the clay when he turned toward her.

"Why don't you come over for dinner?" he continued in a gentle tone. "We're having a barbecue. Ribs."

Stacy shook her head. "I'm really not in a mood to—" She stopped, sat back, and stared at the pot forming on the wheel. "I'm sorry, Pete. I just feel like being by myself for a while. I think I'll stay here and do some work. I might even try to finish up my Tree of Life sculpture."

"You're sure?"

She smiled at him gratefully. "Yeah, thanks, Pete."

"Okay. Hey, how did your first day at work go?"

The smile faded slowly from her face, and Stacy switched the wheel back on with her foot. "It was fine," she said casually, though she felt a little color flood her cheeks. "Nothing to write home about." She darted a quick look at him.

Pete shrugged, and gave her a lopsided smile. "I hope it turns out to be something you like. But don't let that grad student make any moves on you," he quipped. "You know how older men are. See you later, okay?" With a wave, Pete turned and slipped through the door.

Chapter 5

At noon the next day, Stacy was sitting on one of the corner benches in the snack bar, flipping impatiently through the campus paper, drumming her fingernails on the table and waiting for Pete. She looked up briefly when he dropped into the chair across from her.

"Hi," she muttered with a fleeting smile.

"Hi yourself." He leaned forward on his elbows. "Anything earth-shattering in the paper?" he asked, a smile in his light blue eyes.

Twisting her mouth into a sarcastic grimace, Stacy snapped the paper shut and tossed it onto the bench beside her. "There's nothing in it during the semester, and there's absolutely less than nothing in it during the summer."

Pete raised one eyebrow. "However can you

51

stand to stay in this town, Stacy? A city slicker like y'all? You must be going out of your mind."

She managed a thin smile and took a sip of her Diet Coke. "Actually, I haven't the faintest idea how I stand it. I'm surprised myself."

"Let me buy you some lunch to cheer you up, then, huh?" Pete prodded in a cajoling tone. "The chef's special today is caligari."

"Cali*mari*." She corrected him distractedly, and then looked up to meet his questioning glance with a blush. "Sorry. I guess I'm not really very hungry."

He looked at her with obvious skepticism. "You're not starting that no-eating routine again, are you? I thought that was all over with."

"No. Don't worry. I had a big breakfast this morning, that's all."

With a heavy sigh, Stacy poked one index finger at the newspaper. It seemed to consist exclusively of ads for extremely preppy stores, notices for movies, and announcements of picnics and summer school musicals. It all looked so trivial and juvenile to her. People actually went to those Planet of the Apes marathon viewings—and enjoyed them, Stacy noted with an internal shudder. Some of the frat brothers got into it so much they dressed up in chimpanzee masks. In Stacy's opinion, it was a perfect metaphor for Hawthorne College—it was like being on another planet. To her, anyway.

"Stace?"

"Oh, sorry, Pete. I was just thinking of something. She sighed again and forced a smile. "So, how's work going?"

His candid, freckled face brightened instantly. "Great! I know you think it's totally boring to work on a surveyor's crew, but it's good experience for me. It'll help me get into a good engineering program. There's so much competition, and I really need an edge like this."

She nodded politely, but her eyes strayed around the noisy snack bar, looking for a diversion. "That's great, Pete."

"Listen, I'm going to get some food—I only have a few minutes. I'll be right back, okay?"

She slumped back on the fake-leather upholstery, and watched her boyfriend weave his way through the maze of tables and scattered chairs to the counter. *What is wrong with me?* she wondered vaguely. *I don't have the patience for anything anymore.*

As he ate, Pete talked animatedly about the survey he was working on, gesturing with his french fries and arranging salt shakers and straw wrappers to demonstrate lines of sight, transits, and elevations. His enthusiasm carried him through two hamburgers, a plate of french fries, a large soda and a peach.

Stacy stifled a yawn as she listened, wishing she could become more interested in his work. But it was hopeless; she couldn't manage even a glimmer of curiosity. Her eyes down, she picked idly at a rip in the stained seat cushion.

"Well, I've got to go," Pete finished up, wiping

his mouth with a paper napkin. "I'll talk to you later," he added as he stood up with his tray of empty paper plates and cup of melting ice.

"Sure."

He hesitated a moment, looking down at her with a crease of worry between his eyebrows. "Is everything okay, Stacy?"

"Sure. What could possibly be wrong?" she said evasively. She pushed herself up, and hitched her shoulder bag over one arm. "I have to go, too. Mrs. Belasco cornered me the other day and for some bizarre reason I agreed to help her put up a student exhibit in the Fine Arts Complex." She sneered slightly and shook her head as they started walking toward the door. "I must have been suffering from an attack of generosity that day."

"Stacy." Pete put one hand on her arm, stopping her, and looked into her eyes with a tender smile. "You're not as horrible a person as you think you are, you know."

"Don't be too sure," she replied, giving him a wry, lopsided smile. She raised her hand in a small wave. "See you later."

Mrs. Belasco, head of the studio art department, dragged one hand backward through her salt-and-pepper hair, and glanced around with a look that approached panic. A tortoise-shell comb escaped from her disheveled locks and bounced noiselessly on the carpeted floor. "Oh no!" she gasped in her thickly-accented voice. "Those so lovely steel push pins—I have forgotten them!"

"I'll get them," Stacy offered, stepping down from the short stepladder and picking up the comb. "Are they in your office?"

"Push pins. Hmm . . ." Mrs. Belasco scowled at the framed architectural drawing Stacy had just hung. "No, no, Stacy! It must be *so* much higher," she gestured grandly. She plucked the comb from Stacy's hand. "I will in one instant be back!" In a swirl that sent her gauze dress flying around her, Mrs. Belasco marched off down the gallery corridor, muttering to herself.

Stacy shook her head. Mrs. Belasco was the original eccentric artist. She would need at least twenty minutes to find the push pins—that is, if she didn't become absorbed in some new painting. But in spite of her apparent flightiness, when she came back she would still want Stacy to move the drawing higher.

With a shrug of resignation, Stacy smoothed her mini-skirt over her hips, mounted the ladder, and reached up to adjust the drawing. As she wrestled with the wires, she rose up on tiptoe, her arms stretched above her head.

"Nice lines. Very nice lines," came a voice from behind her.

Stacy whirled around, a scathing, ice-cold response forming on her lips. But standing below her, smiling pleasantly, was Carter Cabbot.

"I *beg* your pardon," she drawled with sarcastic emphasis. She hoped her surprise didn't show too much, but seeing him there was completely unexpected, and she couldn't help feeling flustered.

He nodded at the drawing. "Very nice lines on that design," he explained, his brown eyes glowing with amusement. "It's a nice blend of neoclassic and postmodern influences."

For a moment, Stacy looked at him, her eyes narrowed with skepticism. She didn't know if she should laugh or feel insulted. She knew her mini-skirt hadn't hidden anything when she raised her arms—and she also knew perfectly well she had very nice legs. It was obvious that that was what he meant. But at the same time . . .

Stacy managed a smile. "Do you really think so?" she replied flippantly. She hopped lightly down from her stepladder, and stood beside him, looking seriously at the architectural blueprint. If he wanted to play this game, she had plenty of experience in fencing with *double entendres*.

"But don't you think the facade is a little old?" she countered. "I mean, really. Every monument and government building in Washington has that same Greek pediment. It's been done to death."

"No. I disagree, Stacy. I don't think it's old at all. It's really very orginal, unique even," Carter insisted, meeting her eyes steadily.

She arched her eyebrows. "Unique? Derivative is more like it," she said. "Unsophisticated and naive at the very least."

Carter shook his head and folded his arms across his chest. "No, Stacy. Not at all. I think it's all anyone could ever ask for. Perfect, in fact."

As Stacy met his challenging look, she felt her cheeks grow warm and quickly turned away. This was more than she had anticipated! He wasn't all that easy to master in a dueling match like this; in fact, she realized he had just won.

"Well, anyway," she said, busying herself with more framed drawings stacked against the wall. "What brings you to the student art gallery?"

"I like to see what's going on here. I'm fascinated by the artistic mind—the act of creation."

Stacy allowed herself a satisfied smile as she sorted through the drawings, her face hidden. "Do you like sculpture? Pottery?" she asked casually.

"Love it."

"Well, isn't that a coincidence? That's what I do," she told him, feeling extremely pleased by his response.

His eyes widened in surprise. "You're kidding! Somehow I can't imagine chic Stacy Swanson up to her elbows in red clay."

"Well, maybe there's more to 'chic Stacy Swanson' than meets the eye," she retorted with a wry smile.

"I'm sure there is," Carter agreed. He leaned nonchalantly against the burlap-covered wall and fixed her with an amused look. "But clay? I'd have to see it to believe it."

She laughed in disbelief. 'Is that some kind of a challenge?" He waited silently, still grinning. "Well, come to the studio then," she commanded, leading the way. "It's just down at the end of the corridor."

Nodding agreement, he pushed himself away from the wall. "After you."

All the way down the hall, Stacy was acutely aware of him striding right beside her. It seemed natural to be alone with him, though she found herself excited and exhilirated by his attention. With a sarcastic suggestion to herself to get her blood pressure checked, she pushed open the studio door.

"At least you know where it is. That's a start," he teased. He walked into the lofty, light-filled room, looking around in appraisal. Then he hitched himself gracefully onto a stool and looked at Stacy with twinkling eyes. "All right. Let's see what you've done."

Stacy felt a little nervous about showing Carter her pottery. He was so confident about his own work, and she doubted she could appear as sure of her own.

"These are some of my thrown pieces," she faltered, moving dishes and pots around on the shelf. "And I did this vase for a final project."

He examined each piece intently, a frown of concentration on his face. His eyes softened with admiration and he looked at her. "These are really nice. You've got a great sense of proportion."

The compliment went to Stacy's head like a glass of expensive champagne. "You really think so?" she prompted eagerly. She picked up the tall, rounded vase and studied it for the hundredth time. "I worked on this a long time to get the lines right, but I still wasn't sure—"

"It's perfect," he insisted as he took it from her. He turned the vase over and over in his hands carefully, running his fingers along the flared rim. With another smile, he added, "I love these elegant classical forms—there's nothing crude or awkward about them."

Her hand moved protectively to the Tree of Life sculpture she had been working on. She didn't want Carter to see it. It was on the same shelf, covered by a damp rag. Crude and awkward described it perfectly, because that was what she had been aiming for—a more primitive, earthy look.

"Well," she said, her heart thumping in her chest as she moved away. "I'm glad you like them."

"I do, Stacy. I'm very impressed."

She looked over her shoulder at him, a small smile on her lips. "Thanks."

Chapter 6

"Stacy, do you think it's better to say 'extremely significant breakthrough' or 'advance of unprecedented importance'?"

Stacy lowered her hands from the typewriter keys, and frowned thoughtfully. One glance at Carter told her he was sincerely interested in her opinion, and she felt a sudden rush of satisfaction.

"'Advance of unprecedented importance,'" she decided after some hesitation.

Carter shook his head slowly, smiling his appreciation. "Thanks. Your judgment on these things really helps." With a slight flush of pleasure, Stacy turned back to the typewriter.

After a week and a half of working at the psychology lab, Stacy and Carter had fallen into a routine. While he concentrated on preparing his proposal, he often asked for her advice, and he used nearly every suggestion she made. And mingled with the serious discussions about Carter's research were light, bantering conversations that left Stacy with a feeling of exhilaration. For once in her life, she felt like she was contributing to something really significant— and she was having a great time doing it, too.

On top of that was the giant ego boost Stacy got from Carter's obvious admiration. He made no secret of the fact that he was interested in her, in spite of her careful aloofness. Every day since she had started, Carter had asked her out. And each time she managed to turn him down, explaining she had to meet Pete. It didn't seem to put him off, though. When she said no, he would only smile and nod—and ask again the next day.

For a few minutes it was completely silent in the office. Stacy was poring over some notes she had to type up, and when she looked up, she found Carter gazing at her. She raised one eyebrow just a fraction.

"Sorry, was I staring?" he laughed, putting down his pen. He leaned back in his chair and clasped his hands behind his neck. "You know, I can't get over how much I've come to trust you in such a short time."

"What does that mean?"

With a slight shrug, Carter gave her another one of his easy, heart-melting smiles. "It's just that this work I'm doing is so important and I really feel like I need to confide in somebody about—" He broke off, gesturing around the book-filled office. "About everything. The competition for this grant is so heavy, and it's been on my mind for so long."

Stacy smiled softly. "I'm sure you'll get it."

"I wish I had your optimism," he said wryly. "But just talking with you about it helps. Really. It does."

A blush colored Stacy's cheeks, and she turned away in confusion. "It would be the same with anybody," she said lightly, secretly hoping he would contradict her.

"No. It's you, Stacy. I really feel like I can trust you. You're a special person."

Their eyes met, and Stacy nodded slowly. "Well, I'm glad you feel that way." Then, afraid the atmosphere was getting too serious, she added in a heavy accent, "It's warming to my little old heart to feel I am helping somebody."

He laughed and raised his hands in a mock-surrender. "Okay, Stacy. Okay." He bent his head intently over his work again.

A smile lingered on Stacy's lips as she resumed typing. It was nice to feel needed. She would be heartless not to feel flattered, she told herself.

Her mind went back over the past few days, reminiscing about scraps of conversation with Carter. She couldn't deny that he was fun to be with. He was sophisticated, witty, intense, flattering—and sexy. She felt a stubborn urge to repeat it to herself. He *was* sexy. There was nothing wrong with admitting that. Just because she had a boyfriend didn't mean she was blind to other attractive men. Pete didn't expect her to ignore half the population of the world just because they had been dating for a few months.

She dropped one hand to her lap, and fiddled with the gold chain around her neck. It was wrong, but she couldn't help comparing Pete to Carter. There was no question that Pete was caring, honest, intelligent and strong. But there were things about her he would never understand—things that Carter did. For instance, she got a thrill out of mingling successfully at parties for celebrities and politicians; her heart stirred when she watched 'Swan Lake'; and she got a rush when she bought stylish, flattering clothes for herself. She also loved to match wits, which was something that went on between her and Carter every day. With a shrug, she rolled another sheet of paper into the typewriter.

The phone rang, and Carter leaned over to pick it up. "Carter Cabbot."

Stacy had to remind herself that it was ridiculous to like the way Carter said his name in such a self-assured way. She was getting a little carried away with her admiration of Carter; and she was getting absolutely nowhere with her typing.

"Sure, hold on a minute." He covered the mouthpiece of the phone and held it out to her.

"Stacy? It's for you. I think it's your boyfriend." He looked at her for a minute before he let go of the phone.

Her cheeks hot, Stacy held the receiver to her ear and stared blankly at the floor. "Hello?"

"Hi, it's me." Carter had guessed right; it was Pete.

Stacy's eyes darted to Carter. He was watching her steadily, not even bothering to hide that he was listening. "Yeah? I mean—" She broke off, flustered. "Hi."

"How about dinner tonight, Stace? I thought we could go down to Texas Taco and then go to the drive-in, see an old Elvis flick—*Blue Hawaii*. How about it?"

In spite of herself, Stacy felt her attention diverted by Carter again. Her heart pounded as he looked at her. "Dinner?" she repeated faintly. Carter didn't say anything, but he shook his head slowly from side to side and grinned slightly.

Pete laughed. "Yeah, dinner. That's the meal you eat after you eat lunch, and before you go to bed. Remember?"

"Well, Pete," she faltered, looking at the floor and wrapping the phone cord around her finger. "I—I have to work tonight—there's a lot to do." She swallowed hard. *What did I just do?* she asked herself incredulously.

"Work? Are you kidding? Well, okay. If you have to, I understand. I'll talk to you later, though, okay?"

She nodded. "Okay, Pete."

"Bye, Stacy." The phone clicked and went dead.

Carefully Stacy replaced the receiver, avoiding Carter's eyes. Then she pulled her chair back over to the typewriter.

"Stacy?"

She kept her eyes on a page of notes, and forced her voice to remain neutral. "Yes?"

When Carter didn't answer, Stacy had to turn around and look at him.

"Yes?" she repeated in a firm, steady tone.

"We don't have to work tonight."

She matched his ironic expression. "Oh, we don't?"

"No." He paused for a moment, toying with his pen. "If I ask you to have dinner with me tonight, will you say 'no' to me, too?"

Stacy looked down at her hands, pretending to examine her carefully manicured nails. In her heart, she knew perfectly well she had turned Pete down so Carter could ask her out. And she knew it was useless to try convincing herself it had anything to do with work. So far everything about the summer had been boring or disappointing, and she stubbornly insisted to herself it was time she had a little excitement in her life. Carter was definitely exciting.

"I have to admit, you're very persistent," she said with a dry smile.

"I told you, I never let anything get in the way of what I want."

Stacy looked up. "Are you asking me to have dinner with you?" she asked in her most aloof voice. "Or was it just a hypothetical question?"

With a slow smile, Carter nodded. "I most certainly am."

Turning away, Stacy tossed Carter a quick look over her shoulder. "Then I accept."

Maddie hung half off Stacy's bed, a battered copy of *Anna Karenina* open on the floor under her eyes. She reached down to turn a page, and her dark hair swung down into her face.

"*Ooof.* I'm going to cut this all off one of these days," she said. She propped herself up on her elbows and swung her hair back over her shoulder. "You've got the right haircut for this weather."

Stacy nodded silently, dragging a comb through her short, wet hair. Drops of water glistened on her arms and legs, but they were evaporating quickly in the evening heat. Wrapping the towel more securely around her, she opened the closet and stared critically at her clothes.

"Where are you guys going for dinner?" Maddie asked.

"Trattoria Venezia," Stacy replied, pulling a black halter dress from its hanger.

Maddie whistled. "Pete's taking you to that expensive place?"

"I'm not going with Pete." Stacy kept her voice low and her face turned away.

"What?"

Torn between guilt and defiance, Stacy turned around to face her friend. "I said, I'm not going with Pete. I'm going with Carter."

Maddie's face registered total surprise. "You're going out with your boss?"

"Yes, my boss," Stacy repeated with slight sarcasm. She flung off the towel and stepped into her underwear. "It's not a big deal, Maddie. You don't have to act so scandalized."

Maddie swung her legs off the bed and sat up, looking anxiously at Stacy. "Does Pete know? I mean, it's none of my business—"

"That's right, it isn't," Stacy agreed firmly as she slipped the black dress over her head. She gave Maddie a coaxing smile. "Would you tie these straps, please?" she asked, turning her back to her friend. As Maddie silently tied the spaghetti straps across Stacy's tan back, Stacy fought an impulse to shout at her.

"Listen," she said, trying to stay calm. She knew Maddie's questions were perfectly reasonable, and that she was the one who was overreacting.

"Just because I'm having dinner with him doesn't mean anything, okay? We work together, and we thought it would be nice to have dinner together. We're friends. That's nothing to get excited about."

"I'm not getting excited," Maddie shot back, throwing herself back onto the bed. She hugged a pillow across her stomach and contemplated

Stacy for a moment with serious eyes. "Is he picking you up here?"

Stacy returned her gaze steadily. "No, I'm meeting him there."

"Oh." Maddie nodded as though she understood perfectly. "Well, just don't do anything foolish, that's all."

"Foolish?" Stacy laughed in disbelief, and crossed to her bureau. "Listen," she continued as she fastened a string of pearls around her neck. They hung down across her collarbone, accentuating the plunging neckline of her black silk dress. In the hollow of her throat she could see her pulse beating rapidly. She drew a shaky breath. "Trust me on this one, Maddie. I have a little more experience than you do."

Her gaze traveled past her own image in the mirror to see Maddie, who was looking down at the pillow in her lap, her delicately pale skin flushed pink.

"And if you get yourself another room on campus, you'll be able to get a little more experience of your own," Stacy said with more sting in her voice than she intended.

Maddie raised hurt eyes to Stacy's without a word. For some reason, that made Stacy even more angry. "You *are* getting a room on campus, right?"

"Right," Maddie repeated, her voice soft. "Near the library."

"Good. Maybe you'll be able to keep your mind on your work, then, and get all your papers done." Instantly, Stacy regretted her words. The previous semester, Maddie had gotten so busy that she had neglected her term paper for Shakespeare class. In desperation, she had copied Sam's, setting off a chain of events that nearly tore their friendship, and their suite apart. But it had all been settled long ago, and Stacy wanted to kick herself for reminding Maddie of it in such a snide, insinuating way.

Maddie looked at her for a moment, and then pushed herself up off the bed.

"I'm sorry, Mad," Stacy said in a rushed, breathless voice. "I didn't mean anything."

"That's okay. It will be better for me to live in a dorm without a lot of distractions. You're right." Maddie's cheeks were burning pink.

Stacy shot an agonized glance at the bedside clock. "Look, I have to go, Maddie. I'll see you later, okay?" She peered anxiously into Maddie's face, ready to leave but at the same time feeling guilty about hurting her friend like that.

With a nod, Maddie opened the door. "Sure. Have a good time."

Their eyes met, and Stacy felt a slight heat rise up her throat. She turned away. "I will." She waited until she heard the door of the other bedroom close, and then grabbed her shoulder bag and ran from the room.

Chapter 7

Stacy slid into her car and slammed the door. Switching on the ignition, she turned the air conditioning on maximum, and popped a Mozart tape in the tape deck. She sat for a moment, collecting her thoughts while the cool air blew out at her and the strains of a violin concerto filled the car. Maddie's skeptical reaction to her date with Carter had shaken her up more than she wanted to admit.

Outside a couple strolled by arm in arm, their heads close together. Stacy narrowed her eyes as she watched them meander through the parking lot. The girl had blond hair, like Stacy, and her eyes rested on the young man's face: he was tall, dark-haired, and handsome—like Carter.

Stacy felt a rush of excitement as she put the car in gear. She knew that dinner with Carter was going to be fun, and she decided to put all thoughts of Pete out of her mind.

"There's nothing wrong with what I'm doing," she muttered as she drove down a tree-lined street. She consciously avoided the road that would lead her past Pete's house; besides, the route she had chosen was faster anyway. Soon she was speeding along the highway out of town, the speedometer creeping steadily upward as her foot pressed down on the gas.

She turned into the wide, sweeping drive of the stately mansion that had been converted into Trattoria Venezia. The powerful car rolled to a quiet stop at the front entrance. A uniformed parking attendent hurried to her door to help her out.

"Thank you," she said smoothly, conscious of his admiring glance as she dropped the keys in his open hand. She paused for a moment on the steps, watching her Mercedes disappear around the side of the building. Then she squared her shoulders, composed her face into a perfectly cool, poised expression, and climbed the marble steps to the door with leisurely grace.

"*Buona sera, signorina,*" crooned the maitre d', bowing from the waist.

"I'm meeting Mr. Cabbot," Stacy replied, looking past him into the dining room.

The building was a perfect example of Greek-revival architecture, with beautifully proportioned columns and carved moldings. A luxurious blend of muted sounds hummed in the air: a combination of quiet conversation, tinkling crystal and the delicate clicking of silver on china. Waiters glided back and forth with loaded trays like perfectly synchronized dancers.

"If the signorina will come this way," the maitre d' said with a gracious smile. He proceeded her through the dining room, weaving gracefully between tables. Up ahead, Stacy caught sight of Carter, and their eyes met. He stood up as she arrived at the table, and the headwaiter vanished discreetly.

"I hope I didn't make you wait too long," Stacy murmured as Carter pulled out a chair for her. She kept her eyes lowered, not trusting herself to look up yet. She was shocked by the flutter her heart had made when she saw him waiting for her, looking so elegant and sophisticated and—gorgeous. Beside their table a bottle of champagne was cooling in an ice bucket.

He sat across from her, silent for a moment. Then he poured a glass of champagne for her and cleared his throat. "Stacy, I would have waited a week for the thrill of seeing you walk through this restaurant."

"That's laying it on a little thick, don't you think?" Stacy said with an attempt at her usual cynical detachment.

She tried to meet his eyes boldly, and was alarmed to feel her heart begin pounding wildly again. For years, Stacy had prided herself on being able to withstand the most outrageous flattery without letting it go to her head. But for some reason, every word Carter said sent her blood rushing with pleasure.

He laughed. "No, I don't think so. You're probably making every woman in this room green with envy. That dress is a knock-out."

"Thank you," she breathed, looking down.

"Let's have a toast, Stacy," he continued, picking up his glass of champagne. She managed a nonchalant grin, and raised her glass to his. "To Stacy Swanson. One of a kind."

"Thank God for that," Stacy quipped lightly, taking a sip of the sparkling wine. She breathed in the aroma, and let out a blissful sigh. "This is nice champagne. *Very* nice."

Carter leaned back in his chair and a lock of his dark hair fell across his forehead, giving him a boyish look. He was wearing a perfectly tailored gray suit and a red silk tie. "I hope you don't mind, but I took the liberty of ordering for both of us. I've eaten here several times, and I know the chef's specialties."

"No, I don't mind at all. What are we having?"

"I'll let that be a surprise," he teased, meeting her eyes steadily. "They're all things I first tasted in Venice, though."

Stacy drew a deep breath. This was safe territory: She was a pro at travel stories. It was a standard topic of conversation at the high-society parties she went to in Boston.

"When were you in Venice?" she asked casually. She took another small sip of champagne.

"A few years ago. I spent a summer with a friend of mine who has a villa there. A count from an obscure noble family."

Stacy laughed. "Nearly everyone in Italy is from some obscure noble family. I've met a few of them myself. I wouldn't be surprised if the wine steward turns out to be a prince or something."

A waiter appeared suddenly, placing two plates in front of them. "*Tartine*," he murmured in an undertone. "*Mange con gusto.*"

"*Millie grazie*," Carter replied, his Italian pronunciation perfect. He turned twinkling eyes to Stacy. "It's a blend of cheeses, pignoli nuts and basil on toasted bread—I think you'll like it."

Stacy looked with approval at the artistically served appetizer, arranged with sprigs of parsley and black Mediterranean olives on a fragile china plate. With a wry grin, she bowed her head. "I'm impressed."

"Good," he smiled back, then took a bite of tartine. "That's the whole idea. I'm trying to sweep you off your feet, you know."

Stacy couldn't resist a smile of pure delight, and she bit into the savory cheese-covered bread.

"You know," Carter continued, savoring a sip of champagne. "I'd like to see you in Venice. I can picture you in a gondola going down the

Grand Canal, with men throwing themselves at your feet."

"They'd get a little damp if they tried that in the Grand Canal," Stacy shot back, hiding a grin. "No, I like Venice, but after all the place is sinking, you know. In a couple years, all of St. Mark's Square will be under water instead of just a few steps."

"Ah, but that's what makes it so romantic: it's doomed, and decadent, yet beautiful and alluring." He looked at her significantly for a long moment. "That's Venice," he murmured softly.

Carter's comment made Stacy reach quickly for her champagne. She drank quickly, stalling for time while she tried to think of a witty comeback. As she lowered her glass, Carter filled it again.

"And here's our main course," he said. "Angel hair pasta with saffron and veal—*Pasta allo zafferano con vitello.* I think you'll like it."

"I'm sure I will," Stacy replied somewhat breathlessly. The champagne was beginning to affect her head, and a feeling of recklessness stole over her. She caught Carter's gaze and held it for a long moment. In the back of her mind was a cool detached Stacy saying *What about Pete?*, but she ignored it. The Stacy who was sitting in the elegant restaurant wanted to tell Carter how much she liked his subtle—and not so subtle—suggestions.

And besides, the reckless side of her said with defiance, *look at the alternatives: tacos and an*

*old Elvis movie from inside an old pickup truck?
Forget it.* This was the way she had been
brought up, dining in four star restaurants and
talking about European travel and gourmet food
with good-looking, sophisticated men. She
loved it.

She reached for her champagne glass and
raised it to Carter again. "Carter," she said with
a challenging smile. "I'd like you to know I'm
having a wonderful time."

His glass touched hers with a soft, musical
ping. "So am I, Stacy. So am I."

"We'll get our cars ourselves," Carter told the
parking attendant as they strolled out onto the
steps. Bright stars were shining through the
trees, and the soft chirping of crickets filled the
balmy air. Stacy breathed in deeply, a peaceful,
satisfied smile on her lips.

The attendant handed them their keys with a
knowing grin, and they slowly walked down the
steps. In the soft twilight, Carter looked at Stacy
and offered her his arm. Together they wandered around the side of the building to the
parking lot.

The heavy scent of night-blooming jasmine
filled the air and Stacy inhaled again with
pleasure. She knew she was a tiny bit tipsy from
the champagne—and from being with Carter.
Not drunk, of course, but just enough to feel
completely relaxed and carefree. With a blissful
sigh, she tightened her hand on Carter's arm.

"A perfect night," he murmured in her ear. "Mmmm."

Their footsteps crunched on the gravel until they reached Stacy's car. Carter held her back, and Stacy turned to face him.

"Look at the stars," he said, his voice low. "There must be a million of them."

Stacy tipped her head back to look up, and Carter wrapped his arms around her. *He's going to kiss me,* she told herself calmly. *And I'm not going to push him away, either.*

"A perfect night," Carter repeated as he brought his mouth down to hers.

For a moment, Stacy leaned into the kiss, her senses swimming. It was so perfect, so right, a voice inside her whispered. This was meant to happen from the very beginning. But suddenly she remembered Pete, and she stepped back out of Carter's insistent arms, bumping up against the door of the car.

Carter's eyes looked bright and innocent in the semi-darkness. "What's wrong, Stacy?"

Silently she shook her head, trying to clear away the champagne bubbles. It was impossible to keep pretending she just enjoyed Carter's company, and that was all. She knew perfectly well she wouldn't have responded to Carter's kiss if she wasn't—

"Stacy, what is it?" He broke into her thoughts urgently, his hands on her shoulders in a tight, demanding grip.

She stared up at him in total surprise. "I think

I'm in love with you," she said in a dazed voice. Her eyes searched his face anxiously. She could hardly believe she felt it, let alone said it out loud! The cool, aloof Stacy Swanson was head over heels in love.

The worried crease in Carter's forehead eased into a smile. "Oh, Stacy," he whispered as he pulled her toward him again. "You don't know how happy that makes me."

As their lips met again, Stacy knew there was no going back. It was all over with Pete now. Even though she had no idea how she would tell him that, her feelings for Carter were too strong to ignore. She had such intense feelings for Carter. She would do almost anything for him— even if it meant breaking up with Pete.

"Stacy, I'm so crazy about you," Carter breathed into her hair. "I've never felt like this about anyone—ever."

"Me neither." Stacy giggled, feeling as light as a feather. Emotional displays had always been frowned on in her family: She couldn't be as open and spontaneous about her thoughts and feelings as Sam and Roni were. But now she felt like she could say or do anything.

She giggled again. "This is incredible," she murmured, gazing with pure adoration into Carter's eyes. "I can't believe this is happening to me."

"Believe it, Stacy. We've found each other. That's all that counts now. I knew the first time I saw you that I'd never be happy without you."

A quick blush made Stacy duck her head like a shy schoolgirl. "Did you really?" she whispered through a self-conscious smile.

"Mmm hmm."

The crunching of gravel broke into their quiet moment, and Stacy jumped back with a guilty start. For one wild moment she was afraid it was Pete. But it was only a parking attendant coming for another car. He shot them a quick look as he hurried by.

"It's getting late, Stacy," Carter said. "Though I hate to admit it."

She put one hand on his arm. "I want this night to last forever," she breathed softly. She wondered whether he would ask her to come home with him to his apartment: she didn't think she could say no if he did.

With a sigh, he pulled her toward him again. "I wish it could, too, Stacy. But it can't. I still have some work to do tonight."

"Work?" she repeated in disbelief.

He nodded and leaned back against the hood of Stacy's Mercedes. "Yeah, believe it or not. I still have a lot of reading to do. Oh, and that reminds me—" he added quickly, his voice changing to a new, more serious tone. "I have to ask you a huge favor, Stacy."

"Anything," she said dreamily, her eyes roaming over his face, taking in every detail as though for the first time. *This is the man I love,* she told herself ecstatically. *This is the man I'm in love with!*

"Stacy?" Carter's voice was intense and commanding.

"Yes?"

"Listen to me, Stacy. This is important."

She stared into his eyes. "I'm listening," she murmured.

A smile broke over Carter's handsome features. "Okay. What I really need for you to do is when you get back to campus, stop by the psych lab and pick something up for me. I'll need it first thing in the morning. I'd get it myself, but I've got a half hour drive ahead of me in the other direction—"

"Tonight?" Stacy broke in. "But if you need it in the morning why can't you wait? I don't under—"

"Not from my office," he continued smoothly. "It's a file I left in Diane Finch's office—she's another grad student. I happen to know she's going to be in meetings all morning and I don't want to bother her then."

Stacy nodded slowly, a small frown creasing her forehead. "Okay," she agreed hesitantly.

"It's just a file labeled 'Fairmont Day School, September to December.' I left it on her desk a few days ago, and knowing how neat and organized she is, she probably just filed it with her own papers without realizing it was mine. She's like that. Anyway, I'm going to need it first thing in the morning," he stressed again, holding her gaze steadily.

Stacy looked up at him, confused and slightly

doubtful. What he was saying didn't *really* make sense.

He ran one finger caressingly down her cheek. "There's nothing to worry about," Carter assured her, as though reading her mind. "It was a careless mistake, which I'd like to take care of without embarrassing anyone—especially me," he added with a disarming grin. "I even have a key to her office," he explained. "We did some work together last semester, and I forgot to give it back to her. Here."

Stacy stared at the key on her palm. It gleamed faintly in the parking lot lights.

"Room two forty-eight. Second floor, corridor B. Okay? And I do need you to get it tonight."

"Okay," she agreed slowly, still gazing blankly at the key. Her head still felt slightly fuzzy from the champagne.

"Stacy."

She raised her eyes to his, and then put her arms around his neck. She squeezed the key tightly in her fist. "Of course I'll do it. I'll do anything you want me to," she whispered fiercely.

"Oh Stacy, Stacy. I'd do anything for you, too," he echoed, his voice a sultry murmur in her ear. "You know that."

Stacy brought her head back, and they stared into each other's eyes for a long moment before their lips met again.

Chapter 8

Stacy sat for a moment in her car after switching off the engine and stared up at the dark, blank windows of the empty psychology lab. All the exhiliration of being with Carter slowly seeped out of her as she sat there, leaving her alone and slightly nervous. The campus was silent and looked practically deserted.

"Well, it's not as if I'm some kind of burglar, after all," she reminded herself out loud. She twisted her mouth wryly, knowing she was trying to convince herself, and then squared her shoulders and grabbed her small shoulder bag. She pushed open her door and stepped out onto the sidewalk, her footsteps sounding muffled in the heavy, humid night air. The one solitary streetlamp glowed eerily through a halo of mist.

It took several minutes for Stacy to find a door to the building that was unlocked at that time of night. Stacy slipped inside the building like a thin shadow. The hallways were faintly illuminated by the red glow from all the overhead exit signs, but Stacy didn't want to risk turning on the main lighting. She knew she was there for a legitimate reason, but explaining the situation to a security guard might be a little difficult, and it was already late. She just wanted to get the file and get back to Beta House. So she paused for a moment to let her eyes adjust to the darkness. Then she headed for the stairs to the second floor.

The key turned with a soft *snick* in the lock of Diane Finch's office door, and Stacy stepped inside into total darkness. She took a few careful steps and then stopped; she couldn't see a thing.

"Well, this is ridiculous," she muttered testily. I'm never going to find anything without some light. I'll just have to risk it."

Groping forward slowly, she banged into a desk and moved her hands cautiously over its surface until they reached a lamp. Her fingers fumbled up its base for the switch. Stacy let out a sigh of relief as a soft glow brightened the room.

She looked around briefly, wondering if there was some way to tell what kind of person Diane Finch was from looking at the office. The walls were filled with book cases. The desk was neat, with piles of manila file folders stacked at one

side, and a handmade clay cup filled with pens
and pencils stood next to the small, shaded
lamp. Stacy cocked one eyebrow as she admired
the handiwork of the crackle-glazed, hand-
thrown pottery. It was a nice piece, simple but
beautiful, and something Stacy would have been
proud to have made herself. At least Diane Finch
had good taste, even if she *was* careless with
other people's research. Judging from her office,
she seemed to be an orderly, quiet person, yet a
person with assurance and individuality, too.

*Maybe I ought to go into psychology myself if
I'm so good at analyzing people's offices,* Stacy
thought cynically. Then she shrugged, and
turned to the file cabinets. A quick search
uncovered Carter's file, and she nodded decisively.

With one last, lingering glance around, Stacy
slid the heavy drawer shut with a metallic clang,
and hurried to the desk to switch off the light.
Suffocating darkness enveloped her again and
she fought off a momentary sense of panic. Then
the dim rectangle of paler darkness from the
open door became visible, and she hurried
through and closed it firmly behind her. She
leaned against the door, catching her breath in
the silent darkness.

The skimpy, reveal-all black dress she was
wearing made Stacy feel especially conspicu-
ous, even in the quiet, empty building. And her
tiny black shoulder bag wasn't even big enough
for a check-book, let alone a big manila file

folder. She held it awkwardly, wishing she had some place to stow it. Finally she just hugged it to her chest and hurried down the corridor with her head down. She slipped through the exit door again as silently as she had entered, and ran on the balls of her feet around the building to where her car was parked.

Once inside her car again, Stacy glanced quickly at the file, and then tucked it out of sight under her seat. For a moment she sat staring through the windshield at the streetlamp, nervously fingering a short lock of hair behind one ear. She knew she hadn't *stolen* the file, since it was Carter's, but she couldn't help feeling a little furtive, like a thief in the night. Sneaking around at midnight was not her idea of a fun evening, and she couldn't shake off the feeling that there was something peculiar in Carter asking her to do it.

But one consolation was knowing she had done it for *him*. A breathless laugh escaped from her lips as she admitted to herself that she'd probably try to break into Fort Knox if he asked her to. Closing her eyes, she dreamed of just how he would say *thank you*. Stacy indulged in the memory of Carter's arms around her, his lips on her throat. A shiver of excitement and happiness made Stacy's lingering doubts dissolve, and she started the car and headed home.

"Good morning, sports fans! Everyone up! Come on, come on, come on!"

A loud banging—it sounded like an empty coffee mug being rapped on a clock-radio—crashed into Stacy's groggy sleep. She opened one eye warily. Roni was smiling down at her with an angelic look on her face.

"*Good* morning, Stacy. Time for breakfast!"

"Roni, you're going to break either the mug or the clock radio," she muttered grimly as Roni banged again. "Give me a break."

"No, I won't. Come on, get up. Get up! Rise and shine."

Stacy groaned. "Isn't this illegal, Roni? I heard there was a law against chirping before noon."

Across the room, another low groan rose from beneath the rumpled covers on Maddie's bed. Roni's eyes gleamed, and she bounced over to Maddie. "Rise and shine," she bubbled, ripping the sheet and blanket off with one merciless flourish. Maddie let out a feeble yelp and scrabbled frantically for her covers. With a grin, Stacy pushed herself up on one elbow to watch.

"Don't do this to me, Roni," Maddie pleaded in a mournful voice as she lay back on the pillow in defeat. "I can't make my muscles work first thing in the morning. It's not fair."

"Too bad. Does that mean you can't fight back if I start tickling you?"

"No! No, Roni don't!" Maddie shrieked and curled up in a ball as Roni poked her in the ribs. "Don't! Roni, please!" she laughed weakly, trying to roll away.

"Roni," Stacy put in mildly. "You might damage that amazing brain of hers if you're not careful. Then who would correct all your spelling mistakes?" She pushed back her own covers and tucked her knees up to her chin.

Roni stopped abruptly, and Maddie let out a weak gasp. "You're right. I never thought of it that way. Sorry, Maddie."

"What's going on in here?" Sam asked from the doorway. She raised her eyebrows questioningly, and looked from Stacy to Roni to Maddie's prostrate form hanging over the edge of the bed. "Is she dead?"

"Not exactly," Roni announced as she pushed herself up. "But she needs coffee, I can tell."

Maddie moaned with exaggerated despair, and Stacy laughed loudly, suddenly brimming over with happiness. Of all the aspects of being in college, this was the one that meant the most. This was Suite 2C in action.

"The water's boiling," Sam said as she headed for the living room of their suite. "Or as close as it ever gets," she added. Roni bustled out after her.

With a luxurious, feline stretch, Stacy rose from her bed and reached for her bathrobe. "*Mmm.* Instant coffee with generic-brand, non-dairy creamer and artificial sweetener. What a treat." Behind her, Maddie tumbled out of bed and dragged the rumpled Indian print spread around her.

Sam was pouring hot water from a hot-pot into four mugs as Stacy padded into the living room and curled up on the couch. Roni opened a Dunkin-Donuts box and offered it with a grin. "Deep fried crullers—covered in sugar, dripping with grease. *Yummm-meeee.*"

"You really know how to treat a girl," Stacy muttered, reaching for a donut. She took a huge bite and closed her eyes, breathing in the familiar scent of lukewarm, instant coffee and powdered-sugar–covered pastries as she munched hungrily. "I don't know what brought this on, but it's okay by me."

"Yeah, what's with the room service this morning?" Maddie seconded as she reached for a donut and sank down on the couch. Her voice was creaky and faint with sleep, and her eyes were bleary. With her dark wavy hair tangled around her flushed face, and wrapped in the bedspread, she looked like a little girl just up from her afternoon nap.

Sam and Roni and Stacy stared at her for a moment, and simultaneously burst into giggles. An offended look crossed Maddie's heart-shaped face, accentuating the sleepy innocence. "What's so funny?" she demanded in a worried tone.

The others laughed even harder while Maddie's eyes wandered anxiously from one to the other. Stacy put one hand on Maddie's knee. "Sorry, Mad. You just looked so sweet and young—you always seem so pitiful first thing in the morning."

With a snort, Roni popped the rest of a cruller

into her mouth and wiped her hands. "Pitiful is not the word, Lerner."

"No fair ganging up on a helpless person," Sam cut in. She stood up and turned the radio on low, and then threw herself back into her chair. "Anyway, Roni and I went running, and we decided to bring back breakfast. That's all. No mystery."

Stacy chuckled softly. "Roni went running and you say it's no mystery? I think that qualifies for Ripley's Believe-It-or-Not." Roni threw a pillow at her.

"Hey look, she's beginning to wake up," Sam added, grinning at Maddie.

Maddie gave her a pained look. "Ha ha. For your information, I'm completely alert and awake." Roni snorted again and Maddie reached for the pillow in Stacy's lap and threw it at Roni. It hit her squarely in the face as Roni was laughing. "My aim is good, anyway," she added matter-of-factly as Roni yelped with surprise.

"So, when did you get in last night, Stace?" asked Sam through a mouthful of cruller. "I never even heard you come back."

Stacy smiled into her coffee mug as the memory of last night's romantic dinner came flooding back. She raised her eyes and found Maddie looking at her intently. Even though she knew Maddie disapproved of her date with Carter, Stacy was too happy to let it get to her. She set her cup down and looked at her friends with bright, shining eyes.

"Well?" Roni prompted. "You look like you're about to say something momentous."

"I am!" Stacy said explosively. She hugged her knees to her chin, feeling the smile she couldn't control tighten her cheeks. Then she let out a deep breath. "I know you're all going to think this is kind of—I don't know—terrible, I guess. But it's really a wonderful, incredible thing."

Sam's eyes widened. "What? What is?"

"Well, I was out with Carter last night—you know, the grad student I've been working for." Stacy's eyes darted to Maddie, who was looking at the floor. Impulsively, Stacy put her hand on Maddie's arm. "Maddie, don't be like that," she said warmly. "I'm so happy! It's a *good* thing."

Maddie met her eyes silently, and then shrugged.

"Will someone please tell me what we're talking about?" Roni demanded.

Stacy turned to the others. "I know it sounds crazy, but I found out last night that I'm in love with Carter—and I've never been so happy in my whole life!" she finished in a rush.

There was a stunned silence in the room, with just the radio playing softly in the background. Steam curled up from four coffee mugs as Stacy's three roommates looked at one another with surprise.

Finally, Roni let out a long-drawn breath. "Well. Is this really Stacy Swanson talking?"

With an airy laugh, Stacy nodded. "I know, I know. You've never seen me so *un*-cool about myself. But I just can't help it! I've never felt this way, honest! I just can't get over the way I feel. He's so wonderful," she added, turning to Sam with a glowing smile. "He's smart and funny and sophisticated and he makes me feel so great. Now I know what they mean when they say somebody's walking on air. That's how I feel!"

She looked at her friends expectantly, wishing she could share the happiness she felt. It was as though a dam inside her had broken, and all the emotions of a lifetime were pouring out now. She didn't feel like Stacy Swanson at all; she felt like a new person. Her eyes fell on the box of crullers and she laughed again as she took another one, not caring at all how many calories they had.

As she bit into it, she became aware of the uneasy silence around her. Chewing slowly, she looked at each of her friends. She swallowed hard and her smile weakened slightly. "What?"

No one spoke.

"Come on, you guys, what's with you? Aren't you the slightest bit happy for me?"

Finally Roni let out a tiny gasp of disbelief. "Stacy, come on! Just slow down for a second here. What about Pete?"

The smile faded from Stacy's lips. "Oh."

"*Oh?*" Maddie echoed incredulously. Her eyebrows drew together in an indignant frown. "*Oh?* That's all you can say? What, had you completely forgotten about him or something?"

Stacy frowned, too. "Now wait a minute— whose side are you on, anyway?"

"Nobody's on *anyone's* side," Sam put in

gently. Her warm brown eyes were troubled as she met Stacy's hurt and puzzled gaze. "It's just—it seems kind of sudden, and Pete's our friend, too. And you've only known Carter for—like a week, right?"

"Are you sure you know what you're doing?" added Roni with a skeptical look. "Maybe you should wait and see what the second week is like before you go making any big decisions."

Stacy breathed an exasperated sigh. Instead of being happy for her, her roommates only saw the negative side of things. Obviously, there was Pete to consider. But after all, they should be a little more supportive, Stacy thought bitterly.

"Okay, look," she said firmly. "I didn't mean for this to happen, it just did. And obviously I don't *want* to hurt Pete but—" She broke off, meeting her friends' doubtful, uncertain looks. "You just don't understand," she said in a dignified tone. "I thought you might be excited for me, but I guess that's too much to ask." She pushed herself up off the couch, her eyes still meeting their gazes in turn. Then she shook her head and went back to her bedroom.

It's so unfair, she thought angrily as she stripped off her nightgown. *All I want is to be happy, be with Carter and love him. And all I get is grief from them.*

She did have to talk to Pete, she admitted to herself as she sank down on the edge of her bed. She had to break up with him right away—it was the only thing to do. The sooner the better, for both of them. She couldn't lie to him. He would appreciate her honesty in the long run. At least she hoped so.

"I should tell him right now," she muttered out loud. She threw on a pair of designer jeans and a cropped cotton blouse. "I'll go talk to him before I go to the lab—that way I can be with Carter without feeling like I'm being dishonest to Pete."

She glanced quickly at the bedside clock: 8:15. Her forehead wrinkled in a worried frown as she rememberd the urgency in getting Carter the research file "first thing in the morning." She felt torn between settling things with Pete and bringing Carter the file she had promised him.

"Stacy? Phone call." Roni's head appeared around the edge of the door. "In the hall. It's Carter," she added tonelessly.

"Okay, thanks," Stacy replied quickly. She hurried past Roni and through the living room, avoiding looking at her roommates. Her heart was beating wildly as she picked up the phone. "I'm so glad you called!" she said breathlessly. "I miss you."

"Did you get it?"

Stacy blinked. "Yes, but I have to talk to you about some—"

"And no one saw you, no one stopped you, did they?" Carter interrupted urgently. His voice softened as he added, "I've been there at night and it can scare the hell out of you if someone yells down the hall at you."

She shook her head emphatically. "No, there

wasn't anyone there at all. But Carter, there's something I really have to do this morning before I come to the lab—is that okay?"

"No problem—just as long as you have that research material, a few more minutes won't matter that much."

"Oh, good," Stacy breathed. She leaned against the wall and coiled the phone cord around her finger. "I've been thinking about you," she said softly.

"I've been thinking about you, too, Stacy. When do you think you'll be in?"

Stacy stifled a sigh as she remembered what she had to do before she could see Carter again. "I'm going to talk to Pete right now—about us," she said, her voice low. "Then I'll be there and we can be together and not have to think about anyone but the two of us."

"Stacy," he murmured. "I can't wait to see you."

Her heart fluttered wildly, as it always did when she was with Carter. She drew a deep breath. "I'll be there as soon as I can."

"With the file?" he prompted gently.

"With the file," she repeated. "I can't wait till I get there."

"Me either, Stacy. Me either. Come as fast as you can."

As Stacy hung up the phone, she drew a deep breath. No one had ever made her feel the way Carter did. Not even Pete. The problem was, now she had to tell him that in person.

Chapter 9

Stacy stopped the car under a cottonwood tree across the street from Pete's house. She stared across the expanse of green lawn up at the rambling Victorian building for a moment, thinking back to the first time she had ever been there: Thanksgiving Day, last fall.

She had arrived with serious doubts about spending the day with Pete's family. After all, she had hardly known him. She had been dieting compulsively and feeling generally miserable about her life. And besides, Thanksgiving had never lived up to its reputation in her own experience. It had never been a particularly warm or thankful occasion in her family.

But within minutes of walking into the turbulent Young household and meeting a dozen of their friends and relatives, she had been swept up in the loving, joyful chaos, and didn't give another thought to her problems. Getting her out of that pit of self-absorption was one of the most important things anyone had ever done for her, and she owed it all to Pete.

But that stage of my life is over now, she told herself bleakly. *It's time to go forward.*

Gritting her teeth, she opened the door and climbed out into the shade of a cottonwood tree, and leaned against the hood of her car with her hands dug deep in the pockets of her jeans. She glanced quickly at her watch. Pete would be leaving for work any minute now. She had to catch him before he left and get it all over with, get it all out in the open. She felt like her life would be suspended in midair until she did this.

Suddenly the front door opened and Pete came striding out, swinging his denim jacket over his shoulder. She watched silently for a moment, feeling paralyzed and uncertain.

"Pete!" she croaked out hoarsely. She cleared her throat and tried again. "Pete!"

He stopped in mid-stride and looked out toward the street. A big smile broke across his face as he recognized her, and he walked down across the lawn to meet her. Stacy stood rigid where she was, watching him come closer.

"Hi, Stace. What's up?" He leaned against the car next to her, an expectant smile in his twinkling green eyes.

Automatically, Stacy moved away a few

inches, and dropped her eyes from his. She swallowed hard. "Pete, I have to talk to you," she said falteringly. One hand crept up to toy nervously with her hair.

"Sure. Is everything okay?"

For a moment, Stacy looked up into his face without speaking. She could feel her face grow hot, and his open, friendly expression gradually grew wary with a hint of alarm. A frown creased his forehead and Stacy shook her head silently.

"What is it, Stacy?"

"Pete, I—I think we need to talk about something," she stalled lamely. She stared fixedly at a small gray rock by her left foot, clenching and unclenching her jaw as she tried to find the right phrases. Now that she was facing him, she couldn't bring herself to say the essential words.

Next to her, she could feel Pete grow very still and quiet, as though he was holding his breath. An irrational anger swept through her at having to go through with this uncomfortable, awkward scene. She wished she could just tell him goodbye and leave, but she knew there was more to it than that. She owed him a lot more.

"Stacy, why don't you just tell me what you're trying to say? I get the feeling I'm not going to like it, though."

She let out a tense sigh and pushed herself away from the car. She took a few step and stopped.

"I feel like maybe it's time for a change," she said woodenly, pressing her elbows in against her ribs as she crammed her fists into her pockets again. "I—I think I'd like to feel free to—see other guys." She stopped, waiting for his reaction.

Pete was completely silent. Finally Stacy had to turn around and look at him, and the set, stunned look on his face made her heart turn over with an uncomfortable lurch.

"I'm sorry, Pete," she mumbled as a heated flush swept up her throat. "I—things are different now, and—" She gestured futilely.

"Are you serious?"

She nodded. Impulsively she took a step toward him with one hand outstretched, but a short, scornful laugh from Pete stopped her in her tracks.

"I used to wonder how long a girl like you could be satisfied with a boy like me," he said in a tight, unfamiliar voice. "Everyone kept telling me we were too different, and I kept telling them they were wrong, that it didn't matter." He laughed again through his nose, shaking his head. "What a joke on me."

"Pete, that's not—" Stacy broke off, feeling guilty and confused. She turned away again, hating to look at this new, bitter Pete.

"That's not it? Are you sure? You aren't starting to think you can do better than a dumb old hick from Georgia?"

"Oh, Pete, don't say that!"

But a vivid picture of Carter sprang to Stacy's mind, a picture of a suave, cultured man who knew so much about the life-style Stacy was used to. She shook her head mournfully and stared at her feet. "I just think maybe we should stop seeing each other, Pete. I think maybe we're growing apart."

A long, tense pause filled the widening gulf between them, and Stacy fought off the tears that threatened to come. They stung behind her lashes, and distorted the pink and yellow roadside flowers in front of her.

Finally Pete spoke. "There's someone else, right?"

Stacy turned and looked at him speechlessly. His jaw tightened as he read her answer in her eyes. Underneath his freckles, his face turned pink, and then pale, and he turned away.

"I can't believe this is happening," he said softly. His own eyes were sparkling with tears.

"Me, either," Stacy said. Closing her eyes, she leaned back against the hood of her car again. Half of her wanted to stay and sort things through with Pete. But the other half of her wanted to leave, now that she had told him— and go straight to Carter. But she still had strong feelings about Pete, and she knew she couldn't turn away so abruptly.

"Pete, we can stay friends, can't we?"

He turned slowly to face her, and met her eyes levelly without saying anything.

"I don't think so," he said dryly.

"Pete—"

"Listen, Stacy. Let me just tell you something.

When I met you, I thought you were the greatest thing that ever happened to me. I know I pestered you and hounded you till you'd go out with me, but I thought we really had something there—"

"Pete, don't do this!" she pleaded.

They stared at one another for a moment, both breathing unevenly with emotion. Two tears rolled quickly down Stacy's face, and she brushed them away with an angry hand. She knew it was wrong of her to feel impatient: Breaking up with Pete had taken him totally by surprise. But she couldn't help wishing she could just leave now. She folded her arms and stared at her feet.

"Okay," he said quietly. He shifted his jacket from one hand to the other.

"You're going to be late for work," Stacy said. Instantly she regretted her words; it sounded too much like she was trying to get rid of him.

He gave another strange, unfamiliar laugh. "I'm really going to get a lot done today, I can tell you that."

Shaking her head silently, Stacy pushed herself away from the car and opened the door. There was nothing more she could say. She climbed into the car, and stared steadily at Pete, who was still leaning against the hood, not moving.

Then he turned on his heel and walked back up the driveway to where his pickup truck was parked.

Stacy watched him for a moment, and then she turned on the ignition and pulled away down the street, tires squealing. And even though she hated herself for it, she was already putting Pete out of her mind and looking forward to Carter's touch.

The door of Carter's office swung open quickly as Stacy ran into it. It rebounded loudly off the wall, and Carter stared at her in surprise from his desk.

"Oh, Carter!" she wailed, throwing herself into his arms.

"Stacy! What—where—"

She shook her head and pressed her face into his chest. By squeezing her eyes shut tightly, she thought she could wipe out the image of Pete's face just before she left him. Carter's strong arms around her would do it—in time.

"Stacy, calm down. What's wrong?"

Stacy stared up into his eyes. "I just broke up with Pete," she said in a voice deep with emotion.

He nodded. "I see. Come on, sit down," he said tenderly, pulling her toward a chair. He perched on the desk in front of her. "Just relax and tell me all about it."

Swallowing hard, she sat down gratefully and looked up into Carter's eyes. "It was awful, but I had to do it. For us."

"I know, baby. I know." He looked at her for a long moment, and then asked quietly. "Did you bring—?"

Without a word, she handed him her big canvas bag. He took it eagerly, and pulled out the Fairmont School file and gave it a quick, satisfied glance before placing it on the desk behind him.

Stacy shook her head at the memory of breaking up with Pete. "It was awful," she repeated softly. "But I'd do it again for you." As she looked up into his eyes, he reached for her hands and drew her up to him. Her heart was pounding fiercely as his mouth found hers, and she responded eagerly to his kisses. She wrapped her arms around him, and his hands caressed her hair.

"You know," she said with a tiny smile. "If this was a movie, I'd think it was disgustingly sentimental and sappy. But I don't feel that way now."

"I know, Stacy. I know."

She smiled into his shoulder, rubbing her cheek on the fabric of his shirt. "I used to be too cool, too sophisticated to let my emotions show. I guess the way I was raised, it was in bad taste or something," she confessed.

Raising her head, she looked into his eyes. "It's a little frightening, telling you exactly what's in my heart, but it feels right, too." She laughed freely, and threw her head back. "It feels great."

He returned her smile, his eyes slightly mysterious behind his tortoise-shell glasses. For a moment, Stacy wavered. On the one hand, her roommates were right—she had only known him a week or two. But on the other hand, all she needed to know about him was that she loved him. Even though it was a risk to bare her soul to him, she couldn't keep living her life without taking risks.

"I love you so much," she said solemnly.

"I know you do," he whispered, leaning forward to kiss her again. He cupped her face with his hands as he added, "What you did for me last night proves how much—you didn't ask questions, you just did it, even though for all you know, it might not even be my material."

"Don't say that!" Stacy put one finger on his lips, and shook her head with a smile. "I know you would never ask me to do something wrong," she told him. "I trust you completely."

His arms tightened around her. "Oh, Stacy. Together we can go anywhere, do anything. I can feel it! Now that I've got this file back, I can finish the proposal and get the grant money— and then the sky's the limit! We belong together, Stacy. I mean it."

"I know," she whispered, tears of happiness sliding down her cheeks. "I know."

That night, Stacy climbed the stairs at Beta House. She trailed her fingers along the banister, lost in thought. The new emotions that filled her were almost overwhelming, and she could hardly get used to the fact that it was all real. She just wished there was someone she could share her elation with. Unfortunately, she knew her roommates would feel some sympathy for Pete, and would question whether she was doing the right thing. She knew she was. But it would be hard to convince them.

As she passed the little phone alcove in the upstairs hall, she paused. Maybe Sydney . . . Stacy bit her lip in concentration. Now that she felt strong and sure of her emotions, maybe it was a good time to change her relationship with her mother. Maybe she could really talk to her for once, woman to woman. Eagerly she slipped inside the alcove and dialed, using her credit card number.

After four rings, the robotlike recording of Sydney's answering machine came over the line. "This is Sydney. I can't talk to you now. Leave a message—I'll try to get back to you when I can."

Stacy's mouth twisted with a wry smile while she waited for the beep. It was such a typical Sydney message: abrupt, noncommittal, no apology.

The beep sounded just as Stacy cleared her throat. "Hi, Sydney, it's me. I wanted to tell you some good news, so when you get a chance—"

"Stacy!" Syndey's voice interrupted without warning. "Honey, I'm screening my calls. But I was going to call you later."

"That's nice, Mom—"

"Mom? Since when do you call me Mom?" her mother cut in with a dry snort of amusement.

Stacy smiled tolerantly. "I just felt like calling you Mom. You don't mind, do you?"

"Whatever. You can call me Godzilla, for all I care."

Stung, Stacy blinked at the grafitti-covered walls of the phone alcove until an exasperated sigh came over the line.

"Sorry, baby. I didn't mean to snap like that. It's just one of those *days.*"

With a sigh of resignation, Stacy leaned back against the wall and slid down onto the small bench, feeling deflated. She knew that was her cue to ask what was wrong.

I should have known, she told herself sadly. *Why should things be any different just because I'm in love with Carter?*

"Is David giving you a hard time?" she asked politely.

Syndey scoffed. "That miserable—you know, honey, the more I think about it, the more convinced I am he married me for my money. Little did he *know* I haven't sold a painting in months. He apparently thought I was filthy rich."

Swallowing hard, Stacy nodded. She didn't know what to say. But Syndey didn't need any more prompting to keep on talking.

"Underneath his polished exterior—let me tell you, he's nothing but a middle-class hack. He thought that because I live rich I am rich. But once his lawyer took a look at my books he didn't want any part of me or my gallery. Honestly, it's all money with him. He'll be lucky if the court doesn't make him pay *me* alimony!"

For a moment, Stacy was tempted to remind her mother about the trust fund at First Bank of Boston. It was a source of endless amusement to Sydney that because all her assets were in a trust fund, she didn't technically *own* anything. In fact, Syndey bragged about it, and cynically used it as an example of how the rich can get away with almost anything. But her income from the trust was enough for a family to live on quite comfortably. And that wasn't even counting alimony from two of her previous marriages.

Apparently, Syndey had forgotten for a moment that Stacy knew too much to fall for that "poor little rich girl" routine, but it didn't seem to be worth mentioning. Nothing seemed to be worth mentioning to Sydney these days. Just listening to her drained all the energy out of Stacy's body.

"But I don't want to talk about me all the time," Sydney said brightly.

Stacy scowled. *Yes, you do,* she thought.

"You said you had some good news, darling. What is it?"

"It's nothing, Sydney. Never mind. I'll tell you some other time," she replied distantly.

"Well if that's the way you feel about it, I won't press you."

It crossed Stacy's mind that if her mother really cared about her, she *would* press. Sam would. Roni would. Maddie would.

She shook her head with a cynical frown.

"Right. You haven't heard anything from Jason, have you?"

"Your father is incommunicado up in the wilds of Alaska, darling. And he certainly doesn't break radio silence to talk to me," Sydney drawled with heavy sarcasm. "One assumes he'll be back when his supply of twelve-year-old scotch whisky runs out, but who knows?"

Stacy felt a lump rise in her throat. "Syd—"

"Listen, darling. I have to go. Come up as soon as you can. The weather has been heavenly. Bye bye." The phone line went dead in Stacy's hand.

She put the receiver back on its cradle carefully. Another non-conversation with her mother: that was nothing new. She sat staring at a message scrawled in ink on the wall: 'John, party moved to Deke House. Bring the keg.' It was a prime example of the lively fascinating social life on campus.

"This is too much," she whispered, rubbing her palms on her knees. "This is just too much."

But even as she felt herself sinking into a first-class depression, she remembered Carter. If she had to live this life alone, she thought, it *would* be too much. But knowing he was beside her made all the ugly problems insignificant. She breathed a sigh of relief, and gave the telephone a jaunty salute. "See you later, Sydney. At least *I've* got someone who loves me."

Chapter 10

"He loves me, he loves me not." Stacy peeped up at Carter from under her lashes as she plucked the petals off a daisy. She was half afraid he might think she was a total idiot. But he grinned back at her, and she laughed freely as she pulled the rest of the petals off in a clump to land on 'he loves me.'

"I guess it must be true then," she said, tossing the bare stem over her shoulder and leaning forward to kiss Carter. Even after a week of dating Carter, she still couldn't get over how wonderful and carefree she felt: Even pulling petals off a daisy seemed fun and important, and there had been a time in the not-so-distant past when she thought it was the most juvenile, sentimental thing to do in the world.

With a contented sigh, she lay back on the grass, watching a cloud float overhead in the late-afternoon sky. Carter's hand stroked her hair with one hand as he pored over a book.

"How's the writing coming?" she asked with a hint of wistfulness. She craned her neck to look up into his face, trying to read his expression behind his glasses.

He shrugged. "Still hung up on that one spot," he admitted.

"I could help you, you know. I don't feel like I'm being very useful."

"Don't worry—you're an inspiration just being here with me." He looked down into her eyes earnestly, and touched the tip of her nose with a gentle finger. "You don't have to do a thing."

She smiled softly in return, but fought off a feeling of disappointment. Since their relationship had taken on this new dimension, Carter hadn't given her any work to do at all. He kept saying he was having a writing block. But every time she offered to read the manuscript herself and offer a fresh viewpoint, he gently put her off with kisses, insisting that it was too technical for her to help with. She had volunteered to study any book he could suggest to make her more knowledgable about his field. But he kept insisting she was perfect the way she was. That was flattering, but a tiny degree frustrating, too.

Stacy had been feeling somewhat useless, and it wasn't a feeling she particularly liked. But on the other hand, she couldn't imagine giving up the love they shared now. Her days were filled with anticipation, and the nights brought romantic dinners and lazy moonlight walks, stimulating conversation and breathless kisses. No, all things considered, she could stand not being involved with his work now. But she just wished she could share *everything* with him, especially something as important as the grant proposal. All his concentrated energy was targeted on that one goal.

A page rustled as he turned to the next chapter. Stretching, Stacy propped herself up on one elbow and looked out across the lake, watching wavelets ripple as a breeze flitted across the sparkling water.

"Getting fidgety?"

A quick flush colored her cheeks. "No, of course not," she said hastily. "I'm happy just being here with you."

He put down the book. "How about if we take out one of the rowboats?"

"Well . . ." Stacy pulled at a blade of grass, feeling her cheeks grow even redder. She and Pete used to go rowing on the lake almost every week. Somehow she didn't think she could do it with Carter and not feel—like she was doing something mean. She shook her head. "No. Keep on reading and don't mind me."

"If you're sure?"

"I'm sure," she said, smiling tenderly into his eyes. He caressed her cheek lightly and dropped his gaze back to his book.

Stacy lay back on the warm grass, thinking about how lucky she was, and thinking about how ironic life could be sometimes. After all, not long ago she had been regretting staying on campus for the summer, and feeling miserable about Suite 2C splitting up. But then she had met Carter, and everything else faded in significance. All her thoughts and energy went into being with Carter, and she hardly ever even saw her roommates any more not to mention confided in them.

I guess it's like being weaned, she thought, feeling a return to her old cynical detachment. The idea of leaving friends was still painful, but it was getting easier to accept. She felt she could accept anything as long as she had Carter in her life. Maybe next year she would switch from art history to psychology courses—

"Stacy, I have to get back to my place," Carter announced suddenly. "There are some notes there I need to use."

She sat up quickly, and tried to make her voice sound casual. "Need some help?" she asked.

But he was already standing up, collecting his books. "Sorry, not this time," he said with a swift smile. He reached out his hand to help her up, and pulled her into his arms. "But I'll be thinking about you," he murmured.

Stacy's heartbeat quickened at the tone of his voice, but she still felt a twinge of regret. "Okay," she said, trying not to let her disappointment show. "I'll talk to you later, then. Right?"

"Right." He kissed her gently, and brushed her

cheek with one hand. "You don't know how much your help means to me, Stacy. Just knowing you're there for me makes all the difference, it really does. When this proposal is finished and I get the grant, the recognition I'll get from the psychological community will really pay off."

She nodded mutely, not trusting herself to speak. It was worth it, she thought as they turned and walked over the grass to the path. If having Carter meant making certain sacrifices for his work—and it was important work, she reminded herself sternly—then she was willing to make them.

She watched with a soft smile as he climbed into his car and gave her a preoccupied wave. For a moment, she felt a surge of frustration. Carter kept *saying* he wanted to be with her all the time, but it didn't seem to be working out that way. They were together a lot, but sometimes it seemed like he wasn't really aware of her, in spite of the kisses and whispered promises.

Angry with herself for having such disloyal thoughts, Stacy turned and headed across campus. Carter's work was important to him, and she had to accept that. Being second sometimes was just something she had to get used to.

Her footsteps took her in the direction of the ceramics studio, but before she got there she slowed to a halt. She twisted her hair between two fingers, musing. It was nearly dinner time, and it wasn't worth getting all dirty for just a few minutes' worth of work. She realized she had hardly touched her sculpture in a week, but she couldn't manage to work up any enthusiasm for it at the moment.

With a shrug, she turned for Beta House, and let her thoughts drift back into daydreams about Carter.

"Stacy, come on! We want to start." Roni, impatient as always, bellowed up the stairs at seven-thirty.

"I'll be right there," Stacy yelled back as she hitched the shoulder straps of her pink leotard up over her arms. Grabbing a terry cloth sweatband from a drawer, she turned and raced through the suite and down the stairs.

In the Beta House living room, Roni, Sam and Maddie were sitting cross-legged on the floor. They were dressed in the full range of workout clothes, from Maddie's old sweat pants and Northwestern T-shirt, to Sam's running shorts and tank top to Roni's shimmering silver bodysuit. The furniture was all pushed to the edges of the room.

"Sorry," Stacy said, joining them.

Maddie gave her a pained look as she retied her sneakers. "Something tells me I'm going to regret doing this after dinner," she muttered.

"Hey, no pain, no gain," Roni retorted. She crawled across the floor and kneeled in front of the frat's VCR. She pressed 'play' and wriggled back a few feet.

The television screen showed a few seconds

of snow, and then the standard FBI warning against copying copyrighted videos appeared.

"Warning! Warning!" Maddie intoned, robot-like. She waved her arms mechanically, repeating, "Warning, warning!"

Stacy grinned, and stretched her neck muscles. "Let's try to be a little more serious here, Lerner."

A pulsing beat started up, and Jane Fonda's face filled the screen with an encouraging smile. "Ready to start the workout?" she asked brightly.

"No!" Maddie and Sam groaned simultaneously.

Roni shot Stacy a lopsided grin. "Come on, Swanson. Let's show these turkeys how to do it."

For the next twenty minutes the four concentrated on the workout tape. The sounds of the music and Fonda's insistent voice were punctuated by gasps, groans and defeated cries of "I can't," and "Give me a break," from the four girls. Halfway through the workout, Maddie got out of sync with the tape and started giggling helplessly. Sam whipped off her headband and snapped it across the living room, hitting Maddie in the rear-end, which set them all laughing.

Finally, when they were cooling down at the end of the tape, a tired, relaxed silence permeated the room.

"I think I'm going to die," rose faintly from Maddie as she lay flat on her back staring at the cracked ceiling.

"Well, it's been nice knowing you," Sam answered with a weak, exhausted giggle.

"Ha, ha, ha."

Sam let out a tired sigh. "Has anyone besides me noticed how powerful the stale beer smell is from down here on the floor?"

"*Ugh*," gasped Roni, throwing her arms out to her sides. "Go ahead, make me sick."

Stacy smiled to herself as she felt her aching muscles loosen. It was nice to know that in spite of everything, they could still share an evening together without any hard feelings. Even *with* Carter, she knew she would miss these times. But at least she could appreciate them until they were over for good. Looking at their farewell dinner in a new light, it didn't seem like such a bad idea after all.

Roni hoisted herself up on all fours and let her head droop down between her arms. Her auburn curls flopped away from her neck as she turned to peak at Stacy through her knees. "So what's with you lately? You're pretty quiet these days. Anything new?"

Stacy thought for a minute. It occurred to her that there was nothing much new with her. In fact, the more she thought about it, the more clearly she realized that all she had done for a week was wait for the moments when she and Carter could be together. Otherwise, she hadn't really *accomplished* anything. She hadn't looked at it that way before, but that was what it came down to.

"Not much," she admitted, masking the uneasiness and slight embarrassment she felt. "I keep busy."

"Well how's the job going?" Sam joined in. "Still typing?"

Stacy scissored her legs idly above her. "Actually, not very much." She blushed as she confessed, "Carter just likes me to be in the lab with him when he works now, but I don't really do anything. Mostly I just read."

With a short grunt, Maddie pushed herself up and crawled to the VCR. She hit the rewind button and sent Stacy a quizzical look. "Sounds pretty good," she said with a trace of irony. "I wouldn't mind getting paid to sit around reading."

Stacy shrugged, feeling the old, worn carpet scratch between her shoulder blades. It was something she felt a little strange about herself. But she was sure it was just a temporary situation. Once Carter overcame the stumbling block he was sure to make some headway, and she would start typing his rough drafts again. So for the time being, she could just manage to convince herself it was all right.

"Hey, Stace—" Maddie continued as she lowered herself to the floor again gingerly. "I wanted to ask you, did you finish that Tree of Life sculpture you were working on? I can't wait to see it."

For some reason, the question irritated Stacy. Everyone seemed to be checking up on her lately, it seemed. "I don't know," she muttered, rolling over onto her stomach. She propped her chin up on her fists. "I think I may quit ceramics."

There was a shocked silence, and she stared stubbornly at a thread-bare patch of carpet in front of her nose. "It's not as important to me as it used to be," she went on defensively. "I think I'll be taking a lot of psych courses next year, and I wouldn't really have time for the studio—it's too big a commitment."

Roni snorted with ironic laughter. "Stacy, you've never been interested in psychology classes! You were always talking about how bogus my psych assignments were last year!"

"Well, I can change my mind, can't I?"

"But Stacy," Sam cut in quietly. "Do you have to give up ceramics completely? You're so talented at it." She shook her head in disbelief. "I'd love to be able to make the things you do—they're so beautiful."

Their eyes met, and Stacy was touched by the sincerity in her friend's earnest gaze. From the beginning, Sam had encouraged her in her work at the ceramics studio. Maybe she had sensed what a release it was for Stacy to lose herself in the art of creation. Stacy gave her a roommate a tiny, quizzical smile. "Well, I'll think about it."

The front door banged as a group of Beta brothers trooped in. Some of the frat brothers glanced into the living room briefly, saw evidence of aerobic exercise, and fled. The girls exchanged knowing smiles.

"The fastest way to get rid of a guy is say the

word 'aerobics'," Maddie said with a giggle. "It works every time."

"Well, they might start wanting to use their living room, though," Sam suggested in a worried tone.

"They'll get over it," Roni muttered.

Upstairs the telephone shrilled, and was picked up on the second ring. "Stacy Swanson! Telephone!" someone yelled at the top of his lungs from the head of the stairs.

"Ah, frat life," Stacy quipped as she stood up. "Gives new meaning to the concept of civilization." She heard Roni's throaty chuckle as she headed out of the living room.

Wearily she climbed the stairs, and picked up the phone with a sigh. "Hello?"

"Hi, it's me."

"Carter, hi." A blissful smile broke over her face and she sank down onto the floor. "Hi," she repeated in a dreamy voice.

"Stacy, I have to ask you a favor. I've been going over some more of my research for some details to put in the proposal, and I've just realized there's another file I must have left in Diane's office."

With a slight frown, Stacy nodded into the phone. "You want me to go get it?"

"If you would—it would help me so much, Stacy. I can really make some progress once I've got it."

"You know I'd do anything to help—" she began hesitantly.

"Stacy! You're so wonderful! I love you so

much," he cut in exultantly. "You don't know how much it means to me to know you're there, waiting for me and believing in my work. I know I've been acting like a selfish bore lately—"

"No you haven't," Stacy interrupted, filled with tender forgiveness. The momentary twitch of uncertainty that had surfaced at the mention of going back to Diane's office sank into oblivion. "Of course I'll do it, you know I will. What is it filed under?"

She heard Carter sigh with relief at the other end of the line. "It should be labeled *Candlewood Day Care, Timed-Response Experiments*."

"Do you want me to bring it to you?" she asked with a surge of hopefulness.

"No—that's not necessary."

"I wouldn't mind," Stacy said eagerly.

"No, Stacy. As long as you get it tonight and bring it with you in the morning, that's fine. We can work by the lake again tomorrow if you want."

Stacy swallowed. Another day at the lake meant another day of not doing anything except work on her tan. And being there for Carter, she reminded herself a second later.

"All right. I'll get it."

"Thanks—you're the best, Stacy. You're so good to me."

With a breathless laugh, Stacy leaned back against the wall and closed her eyes. "You really have a way with words," she sighed happily.

"You can turn me into the most sentimental blob of spineless Jell-o. And I love it!"

Carter's rich laugh sounded over the line. "I'm glad to hear it," he said lightly. "Not how about getting over to the psych building before it gets too late?"

"Okay. I'll go right now. See you tomorrow."

Still smiling, Stacy hung up the phone and stepped out of the phone alcove just as Roni reached the landing.

"Hey, Davies."

"Hey, Swanson," Roni echoed with a grin.

Stacy swung her sweatshirt across her shoulders, filled with contentment. "Want to go across campus with me for a minute?"

"Sure, I was going to take a walk anyway. Let me put on some sweats."

Humming softly, Stacy followed Roni into their suite and grabbed the key to Finch's office from her jewelry box. Out in the living room she rejoined Roni and the two trotted down the stairs and out into the twilight.

"Where are we going, anyway?" Roni asked as they turned down the path toward the Science Complex.

"Psych lab—I have to pick up something for Carter for work tomorrow."

"Work—hah!" Roni scoffed breezily. "Some night, huh? Too bad we're not hard at work studying instead of relaxing and doing nothing, isn't it?"

Stacy laughed and nodded. "A real shame."

They were silent the rest of the way, not

feeling the need to speak. Stacy was glad they could still do that. No one had said anything lately about housing for the next year: it was as though that subject was off limits. No one wanted to bring up an uncomfortable topic of conversation to ruin their last weeks together. It was only two weeks before Stacy was planning to go up to Nantucket.

Their footsteps echoed in the empty hallway as they climbed the stairs to the second floor in the lab. Roni leaned against the wall while Stacy fiddled with the key in the doorknob. When it released, Stacy pushed open the door and stepped inside, reaching in the darkness for the desk lamp.

"So, this is where you don't do work with the notorious Carter Cabbot," Roni drawled as she followed Stacy inside.

Stacy paused, one hand on the file cabinet handle. "Actually, this isn't Carter's office."

"It's not? Whose is it, then? And why are we here?" Roni's voice registered mild surprise. She had a reputation for pulling a lot of pranks and practical jokes, and would go to any lengths to fulfill a devilish plot.

But Stacy felt a certain reluctance to explain, and she began to regret inviting Roni to come along. "It's Diane Finch's office—Carter left something here that he needs," she said casually. She yanked open the drawer. When Roni let out a low whistle and didn't say anything, Stacy turned around. The expression on her room-mate's face gave her a jolt. "What?"

Roni shook her head in disbelief. "Stacy, don't you—" She broke off, still shaking her head. "I guess you wouldn't know since you were never in the psych department during the school year. I was going to tell you, but I figured it didn't really matter anymore."

"What? What didn't matter?" Stacy demanded. She cast a quick look toward the open door as Roni hopped up on the desk.

Drawing a deep breath, Roni explained, "There was this big scandal last semester—I heard that your lover boy Carter Cabbot and Diane Finch were a hot item, and they were working on some big research project together."

Stacy swallowed with difficulty. Carter had never mentioned anything about it. She cleared her throat. "So?"

Roni shrugged and toyed with a pencil, bouncing it on her open palm. "I don't really know the official story. But I heard she accused him of rigging some important data—or maybe he accused her." She shrugged again and dropped the pencil back into the pottery cup. "Anyway, they split up and went their separate ways. They're supposed to hate each other's guts and be professional rivals now. So it seems strange he asked you to get something from her office. I mean, it figures he wouldn't have been caught dead here, let alone leave his research laying around."

Stacy's mouth felt as dry as a flour sack, and she could feel her cheeks heating with a fierce blush. Roni was looking at her quizzically, waiting for her to say something. Turning away quickly, Stacy felt her mind spinning. Obviously, Carter hadn't given her as full an explanation as he could have.

Maybe he didn't want her to feel any jealousy about Diane Finch. Stacy grabbed that thought and hung on to it for life. That's all it was, definitely. Carter cared too much about her to want her to be hurt by a silly story like that. Besides, campus gossip was notoriously wrong. Wasn't it?

Behind her, Stacy heard Roni hop off the desk. She searched frantically for the file, and found it, relieved. As she turned, she fought to put a nonchalant expression on her face.

"Oh, that," she glibly, pushing the drawer shut. "I knew about that—it's just that he had left this file here and he needed to use it. That's all." She met Roni's doubtful gaze steadily. She even managed an unconcerned smile. "That's all," she repeated lightly as she led the way to the door.

Roni reached for the lamp to turn it off, and gave Stacy one last questioning glance before darkness blanketed the office. The moment it did, Stacy felt her smile wilt. She *believed* in Carter. She just wished he had told her the truth.

Chapter 11

Stacy sat down carefully on the grass, pulling the bottom hem of her denim mini-skirt down a bit as she curled her legs underneath her. Then she took a deep breath and tried to arrange her face into an expression that would convey—what? Expectation, disappointment, hope? Her mind had been spinning since the night before. There had to be a reasonable explanation for it all. There must be.

Her big canvas bag was on the ground next to her, and the research file from Diane Finch's office was inside it. Carter's research file. At least, she had to assume it was his—she only had his word on it.

Stacy felt a wild surge of sickening panic go through her. It was hardly possible, but somehow could she have made a huge mistake? Had she been acting incredibly stupid? A wave of heat that didn't have anything to do with the rising temperature washed over her, and the lake blurred in her vision. *No. Absolutely not. He couldn't have*, she told herself.

Turning her head, she saw Carter approaching, and she caught her breath. He looked so great: striding along with such confidence, the sun glinting off his hair. Wearing white shorts and a red polo shirt, he looked even better than usual. She could easily imagine him as the skipper on an ocean-going yacht, or smashing ace serves on the tennis court. A smile quavered on her lips, and her heart began beating faster.

He smiled a greeting as he joined her, and kneeled down beside her to place a soft kiss on her lips. Sitting back, he looked into her eyes.

"Did you get it?"

She dropped her eyes in confusion, and placed her hand protectively over her bag. She felt an overwhelming reluctance to turn it over before she had an explanation—*some* kind of explanation.

"What's wrong? Didn't you—" His eyes were troubled, and his strong brows drew together in a frown. "Stacy, didn't you get it?"

"Ye-es," she admitted slowly. "It's just that . . ."

"That what, Stacy?"

Finally she looked him squarely in the eyes and spoke bluntly. "I heard you and Diane Finch used to have a serious relationship, and that you split up over some kind of accusations or disagreements." Swallowing hard, she searched his face for some unmistakable sign of guilt or innocence. "Is it true?"

His jaw clenched tightly, and he folded his arms across his chest with an irritated sigh. "Who told you this?"

"It doesn't matter who told me," she whispered. She turned away and looked at the geese on the lake. She forced her voice to remain neutral. "Is it true?"

There was a long pause while Stacy held her breath. At last Carter let out another long sigh. "Yes, it is."

"But why didn't you tell me?" Stacy was horrified to hear a whine creep into her own voice, but she couldn't help herself.

"Stacy, Stacy." He shook his head wearily, and touched her arm with a gentle caress. Leaning back on his elbows, he stretched his long legs out on the grass and stared at the water with a deeply sorrowful expression.

"Okay, I guess I should have leveled with you in the beginning." She turned to look at him with pain in her eyes as he went on in a low, serious tone. "Yes, Diane and I were involved, and we were working together on a big project. But I started to get the impression that she was a little—I don't know, unbalanced, maybe?" He broke off, looking very sad.

Stacy nodded wordlessly, encouraging him to

go on. She plucked absently at blades of grass near her feet as she listened to his story.

"Anyway, maybe that's too strong a word, but at any rate, I started to back off a little. She made me very nervous, and I didn't want to jeopardize the work. I started to think maybe it was more important to her to see how she could manipulate people than it was to go through with the project."

With another tired shake of his head, he met her eyes. "When she realized I wasn't taken in by her any more, she started making these wild accusations, making up these bizarre stories about how I was falsifying my data! As if I would.

"And now—well, obviously, I stopped working with her, but she still had a lot of my files. I asked her to give them all back, but I realized she had held on to some of them. On purpose, I'm sure."

Frowning in concentration, Stacy asked, "You mean, to use the research herself?"

He shrugged hopelessly, a look of utter sadness and pity in his brown eyes. "Who knows? Probably that, or to use as a lever against me. I can't understand how her mind works, I really can't."

"I see," Stacy replied slowly, gazing out across the water again. It was a sad, pathetic story, and it made her furious for Carter's sake. At the same time, though, it didn't quite sit with the impression of Diane Finch that Stacy had formed in the woman's office. It was hard to believe that Diane

Finch could be such a jealous, vindictive, spiteful person and yet have an office which demonstrated such reasonable, well-ordered calm. With a silent, self-mocking laugh, Stacy reminded herself that she wasn't always the best judge of character.

"And you can understand why I would want to avoid going to her office myself," he added quietly. He looked out at the water again, his jaw muscles working.

Stacy reached impulsively for his hand. He seemed so genuinely sad about it, rather than angry or revengeful. With a reassuring squeeze, she smiled tenderly at him. "I do understand. I— I just wish you had told me before, that's all."

"I know, Stacy," he confessed with a rueful, boyish smile. "But I didn't want you to hear such a sordid story—it sounds dumb but—" He broke off, suddenly shy.

"But what?"

He gave her a sheepish grin. "I guess I didn't want you to worry about, well, having any kind of lasting relationship with me or anything like that. Because *we* can have one, Stacy."

A lump rose in Stacy's throat as he spoke. The misunderstanding had all been a result of him trying to protect her. And in spite of the lavish, privileged life she had lead, she couldn't remember anyone ever trying to shield her from unpleasantness before.

"You're so good to me," she whispered in a choked voice. She drew the file out of her bag with a trembling hand and held it out to him. With a sigh of relief, he sat up and took it from her. He flipped through it rapidly.

"I'm just sorry it had to happen to you, that's all. But Carter?" she added, a note of uncertainty creeping back into her voice.

He dragged his eyes from the file which he had taken so eagerly. "Yes?"

Stacy looked away, and licked her dry lips nervously. Suddenly the heat had become very noticeable; in spite of the fresh morning breeze, the humidity was rising fast, as was the temperature. It was going to be another blistering day.

Willing herself to keep cool, Stacy drew a deep breath. "That was the only file left, wasn't it? I mean, you know I don't mind having gotten it for you, but I'd rather not have to go again," she confessed warily.

"Don't worry, Stacy." He reached one arm across her shoulders and drew her to him. "As far as I can tell, that's the last one."

"Because if Diane found out, it sounds like she's the kind of person who would make trouble, given the chance," Stacy continued.

"It's okay, really. You won't have to do it again, Stacy." He kissed the top of her head. "But I'll never forget what you did for me. You know that, don't you? When I win this grant, it will be because of you. Standing beside me, supporting me, loving me—you've made it all possible."

Stacy nodded, not trusting herself to speak with her emotions in such turmoil. How could she ever have doubted him, she wondered with surprise and happiness. She didn't know whether to cry with relief or laugh from the satisfaction of knowing how much he loved her. All she knew was that when she was with him, she felt swept up in the force of his personality, and she had no choice but to follow him and love him. It was frightening, but at the same time it was exciting, too.

"And when I write my first book," he went on in an emotional voice, "I'll dedicate it to you."

Stacy looked deep into his eyes. Whatever happened, she knew she would always love him more than anybody else.

Stacy wandered idly back to Beta House after having dinner with Carter. After a long day spent at the lake watching him write, Stacy had been relieved and happy to go with him to the Dixie Diner. Then they had returned to the lab so Carter could get back to work. But in spite of her protests, he had insisted on her going back to the frat, saying he needed to be alone. Her lips curled up in a dreamy smile as she recalled his words.

"With you here, all I can think about is how much I want to get my arms around you, Stacy," he had said, smiling broadly. "You're too tempting a distraction. I'll just have to be a monk and go into seclusion for a while."

With a throaty chuckle, Stacy swiped at a bush as she passed along the tree-lined shortcut to Beta House. Pulling off a sprig of heavy-scented blossoms, she held it to her nose and paused, inhaling deeply in the darkness of the path. It had been a long, hot day, and the heat was still a strong, inescapable weight. She sniffed the blossom again, tipping her head down to catch what breeze there was on the back of her neck.

"All I know is, Stacy is acting totally bizarre." It was Roni's voice, coming clearly through the bushes. Stacy froze. Apparently her roommates were sitting on the lawn behind the frat house in the twilight. They were just yards from where she stood concealed in the darkness of the overhanging branches.

Sam's voice joined in. "I know," she said in a worried tone. "Do you think we should say something to her? I mean, that stuff you told me about taking research files from that woman's office—it sounds weird."

Indignant, Stacy clenched her fists. Who asked Sam to like it, approve or disapprove? And for that matter, what gave Roni the right to blab about her personal business anyway? Fuming silently, Stacy decided to step through the bushes and give her friends some much needed advice on the merits of minding their own business. But something held her back.

"I doubt it would do much good to talk to her anyway," Maddie added next. Her voice sounded more distant than the others', as though she was lying on the ground and speaking to the trees

overhead. "Lately she's been so spacey, I keep
wondering if she even hears me when I say
something to her."

"Yeah," Roni drawled. "Spacey Stacy. I get the
same feeling, like she's not really there."

"Well, it burns me up to see her like that."
That was Sam again, Stacy realized, as hot
waves of anger and hurt washed over her. "You
know, I've always admired Stacy for being so
independent and in control—always knowing
what she wants. And now—I hate to say it—but
it's like when she's with us, she's sort of on hold.
You know? Like she's only plugged in when she's
with this guy Carter."

Maddie agreed. "That's right. She doesn't do
anything when she's alone now. She just waits
for him."

"I can't believe she isn't doing any sculpture
anymore, either," Sam went on, her voice rising
in pitch. "How can she just completely lose
interest in it? It was always so important to
her—even when things got crazy around here
last year."

Off in the distance, there was a low rumble of
thunder, and the breeze began to pick up a little.

"I can think of a reason." Roni's voice was sarcastic, but she sounded worn out, too. "Carter.
He's turning her into a zombie."

Stacy felt her mouth drop open. That wasn't
how it was! She wasn't a zombie! She could
hardly believe she was hearing this from her

roommates. Was that really the way they saw her? She wasn't totally spaced out.

But on the other hand, she had to admit that there was at least a grain of truth in what they were saying. The sprig of blossoms twisted in Stacy's fingers as she stood there, musing. Perhaps she had been acting a little dreamy lately, she admitted reluctantly. And considering how she used to be—cool, cynical, wry, blasé— it must seem like a pretty drastic change to her roommates.

But there wasn't anything wrong with being softer, gentler, more contemplative. She swallowed, and clenched the tattered sprig in her fist. It wasn't spaciness—she didn't just sit and wait for the moments when she and Carter would be together. Or did she? The truth was, since she had met him, she hadn't done a thing. She hadn't touched her sculptures, or opened a book, or gone on a day trip—all on the off chance that Carter would need her.

Sam's voice suddenly broke into her reverie again. She craned her neck to listen above the rustling of leaves in the wind.

". . . And I don't know what to say to him. I felt so bad!"

"Did he say anything about Stacy?" Maddie queried.

"Not really. He was kind of embarrassed—I can't blame him—but jeez! Why should we suddenly have to stop being friends with Pete just because Stacy dumped him?"

Stacy's insides twisted sickeningly. Half of her wanted to leave, but the other half of her was holding her hostage, forcing her to listen.

There was a creak of a lawn chair, and Roni spoke again. "You know, once last semester I was somewhere with Pete—I don't know, maybe it was the library or something. Anyway, he was telling me that what he admired the most about Stacy was that she could be in charge and make decisions so well—and if there was something she wanted to do, she just went ahead and did it, alone if she had to. That she didn't need to sit around waiting for him in order to have a good time."

"Well he wouldn't recognize her now," Maddie put in, her voice surprisingly hard.

"I know," Sam agreed with a sigh. "It just doesn't make any sense the way she broke up with him right out of the blue. She's always been the one with the coolest nerves. I mean, she never used to rush into important decisions. She was always so calm and objective about things. I know sometimes she seemed almost cold about things, but a lot of that is just a defense mechanism for her."

Through the trees, a flash of heat lightning flickered along the horizon. The air suddenly felt cool on Stacy's cheeks, and she realized there were tears running down her face. Hearing the story from her roommates' point of view made her realize how blunt she had been with Pete.

Thinking about it, she knew she had acted irresponsibly. She had probably been cruel, too.

Stacy wished she could just curl up in the soft grass under the trees and make all her feelings of guilt and confusion go away. She didn't think she could stand to hear anything else her roommates might have to say about her. On tiptoe, she backed down the path quietly and skirted around Beta House to slip in the front door unseen.

Another roll of thunder drummed a low, distant rumble that Stacy could feel in her breastbone. There was a storm coming, but it was still far away. She wanted to be in bed, pretending to be fast asleep, before her roommates came inside.

But as she climbed softly up the stairs, the phone rang in the alcove. She debated for a moment whether to answer it. If it was for one of her friends, she'd have to go get them, and she didn't think she was up to facing any of them at that moment. Pressing her lips together, Stacy looked up and down the hallway to see if anyone else was around. Beta House seemed deserted, as usual.

With a sinking heart, Stacy picked up the receiver. "Hello?"

There was a short pause. "Stacy? Is that you?"

"Oh!" A surge of relief pulled a heart-felt sigh from Stacy's lips. "Carter," she whispered, close to tears. "Hi."

"Hi. Listen, I hate to do this to you—"

She felt her stomach muscles tighten. "What?"

"Stacy, there is one more file that Diane must have in her office. And I need it, desperately. There's no getting around it."

Stacy stared blankly at the hall carpet outside the phone alcove, following the worn path trampled through it over the years. She couldn't bring herself to say anything.

"Stacy? I wish there was some other way to do this, but now you know why I can't take a chance of getting it myself, right? If anyone saw me go into her office, they'd be suspicious immediately. Everyone who works in the building knows about it."

"Oh Carter, do I have to?" Stacy asked. She sounded like a reluctant little girl. "I really—"

"I know you don't want to, Stacy. And believe me, if there was some other way . . ." He trailed off, his tone implying that she had no choice.

Nodding wearily, Stacy drew a deep breath. "All right," she said woodenly. "I'll do it."

Stacy could almost see the smile of triumph on his face as he gave her the name of the file. Knowing how happy she was making him was only slightly comforting this time. "And I'll be here in my office, waiting for you, Stacy."

Chapter 12

Heat lightning flickered and shimmered all over the sky as Stacy jogged across campus. The dull drumroll of thunder boomed slightly louder, and above her, the tree branches started crashing together in the wind. She ducked her head and sprinted a little faster, hoping she could outrun the storm.

Over and over in her mind ran the words, *the last time, this is the last time,* and she urgently hoped that they were true. Even so, she felt an almost paralyzing reluctance to enter the lab when she got there. She stared up at the building, afraid to move. Way down at one end a light showed in an office: Carter's.

"I'll give it to him, and then just tell him how I feel," she muttered, hugging her arms around herself. "I'll tell him how important it is to me to feel like I'm accomplishing something, instead of just sitting around." Although she didn't like to admit it to herself, she knew she was guilty as charged by her roommates.

As of right now, she decided, she'd pull herself together. There was no reason why she couldn't be herself and still have Carter. She hesitated for a moment, contemplating the idea. She had broken up with Pete so she could be with someone who came from the same background she did, so she could be true to her nature. In fact, though, she had been much more herself with Pete. But she squelched that thought as quickly as it had popped up.

She nodded decisively and pulled open the door. Taking the steps two at a time, she bounded upstairs and down the corridor, pushed by an overpowering sense of urgency. Maybe it was the approaching storm, or the shame and guilt that kept returning whenever she remembered the conversation she had eavesdropped on, but she felt like she simply had to get the file and get out. Fast.

Her hands fumbled with the key in the door, but once it was open, Stacy darted inside and flicked on the lamp. Without pausing she dragged open a file drawer and began rifling through the tabs, searching as fast as she could. Her breath was coming in short, tense gasps.

"What are you doing in here?"

Stacy whirled around, stricken with fear.

Standing in the doorway was a tall woman with wavy dark hair. The woman regarded her calmly but curiously. Her attractive face was composed and noncommittal, but there was a hidden strength of character there under the surface. Stacy knew instantly she was looking at Diane Finch, and in spite of her pounding heart and jumping nerves, she was conscious of the fact that Diane hardly matched the image of a wild-eyed psychotic that Carter had painted. In fact, she was much more like Stacy had initially imagined her to be.

"What are you doing?" Diane repeated, folding her arms across her chest. She looked pointedly at the file cabinet. "Why are you going through my files?"

"They're *not* yours," Stacy blurted out, suddenly spurred into action. She drew the file out with a defiant flourish. "I'm returning this to the person it belongs to," she added, meeting the woman's eyes unflinchingly.

Looking surprised, Diane cocked her head to one side. "Really? And just whom does that file belong to?"

"Carter Cabbot, as if you didn't know," Stacy sneered, clutching the folder to her chest. She was trembling slightly, and she tried to force her body to remain still.

"Carter Cabbot." Diane's mouth settled into a stern line as she crossed to her desk and sat down. "Would you like to explain that, please? I'm sure you can understand this comes as a shock to me—finding out that my research data is really someone else's," she commented dryly.

A vague feeling of uneasiness stole over Stacy as she listened to the woman's level tone. She had expected heated denial or angry defiance, not this cool, slightly sarcastic self-possession. She wet her lips nervously.

"Well, everyone knows you two used to work together and when you split up you held onto his research material so you'd have some kind of hold over him," she faltered, her voice weaker than she wanted.

Diane Finch said nothing. She stared into Stacy's eyes.

"I don't know what happened between you, but he said he didn't trust you, and he was afraid you wouldn't give his data back," Stacy went on. Her eyes darted to the open doorway, and back to Diane Finch. "He had no other way to get it so he asked me to do it for him."

With a tired sigh, Diane rubbed her forehead and stared at her desk blotter. She rearranged some paper clips by fiddling them into rows with one slender finger. Then she looked up sharply at Stacy. "Are you in love with him?"

Stacy widened her eyes in surprise. She wondered briefly if Diane Finch was jealous, but something told her instantly that that wasn't it. "Yes, I am," she retorted, raising her chin. She added, with all the haughty dryness she could muster, "Not that it's any business of yours."

The woman shrugged slightly, as if it didn't

matter much one way or the other. Her calmness came as an impressive surprise to Stacy, who had seen many people try to maneuver their way through tricky situations before—with little or no success. "What's your name?" Diane asked.

"Stacy," she replied faintly.

Diane rubbed her forehead again, and met Stacy's eyes with a look of compassion. "Listen, Stacy. I've got to tell you the truth about our Mr. Cabbot. And I'm afraid you're not going to like it very much."

Stacy returned her look coldly. "Go ahead. I won't believe you."

"I hope you will," the woman stated simply. She examined her fingernails for a moment, and then said, "Carter Cabbot is man with driving, all-consuming obsessions. I don't know how to put it any more simply than that. And more than anything, he's obsessed with winning fame, with people looking up to him with awe and respect. Right now that means getting this grant money, and he'll do anything for it. Anything."

Stacy tried to keep her eyes focused on the woman's face. *I don't believe you,* she wanted to say, but the words didn't quite make it out of her mouth.

"He's using you, Stacy. Just like he tried to use me when we were together. And like he's trying to use my work," Diane added wryly, nodding at the file in Stacy's hands. She shook her head sadly. "Believe me, he'll do anything for that money."

In the back of Stacy's mind, she heard a faint, nightmarish echo of her mother's voice saying exactly the same thing—about David. David, with whom Sydney had been so infatuated. Sick with anxiety, Stacy recalled thinking that Carter was just her mother's type.

But as the recognition flashed through her mind, her love and loyalty came fighting back to the surface. She felt like a traitor for thinking that way. She had to believe in Carter. She *had* to.

"I don't believe you," she finally whispered, staring desperately at the filing cabinet.

The older woman shrugged again. "I'm not surprised. He's pretty persuasive. I know that from personal experience." She spoke softly, as though to herself. Then she shook herself and met Stacy's eyes with more determination and sternness. "I suggest we go ask him for his side of this little story, then. We'll see what he has to say for himself."

"No!" Stacy shook her head vehemently, her defiance giving her a new burst of courage. She met the woman's eyes with a look filled with scorn. "I don't need to prove anything!"

"Actually," Diane said harshly, "you do. I have caught you in my office in the process of stealing my files. I think you would have quite a lot of proving to do to campus security."

As Diane reached for the telephone, Stacy felt

her strength draining from her. It was true. She didn't have a leg to stand on, no matter what the real story was. She had been caught red-handed, committing a theft. She wondered dully how she could have overlooked that fact all this time. All she could pray for was that Carter would make it all right again, that he would come to her rescue and stop this nightmare from getting any worse.

"Okay," she conceded, trying to marshall her forces. She met the woman's eyes and hoped she wouldn't make a fool of herself by bursting into tears. "We'll ask him."

Diane's stern expression softened, and she nodded slightly. "I'm sorry to do this to you," she said, beginning to dial. "I'm going to call security anyway—I'd like to have an independent witness to hear what Carter says." She paused for a moment before she finished dialing and glanced up at Stacy. "To tell you the truth, Stacy, my guess is, when he's cornered all he'll do is try to save his own skin."

Stacy swallowed painfully, not wanting to believe Diane.

"He'll throw you to the lions."

Three pairs of footsteps echoed along the corridor. Diane Finch had spoken quietly but firmly to the campus security guard who had come to her office.

"All I'd like is for you to listen to a conversation, officer. I don't want you to make any judgments ahead of time, so do you mind if we just leave it at that?"

Trailing behind the others, Stacy folded her arms across her chest. For a moment, she fought a wild temptation to run ahead of them to Carter's office, to warn him, give him time to prepare. But the part of Stacy that was trying to stay detached and in control reminded her that Carter didn't need to be warned—if he was innocent.

Diane Finch knocked briskly on Carter's door, and Stacy shrank back into the shadows as she heard his voice call, "Come in."

Diane gave her a quick, compassionate look, and led the campus security guard in. Inching toward the open door, Stacy strained her ears to hear what was being said. She fixed her eyes on the shaft of light that fell through the doorway into the hall.

"Diane, this is a surprise," Carter said. "Is there a problem, Officer? What can I do to help?"

"Carter, my office was broken into tonight. That's why he's here. I thought you should know."

There was a pause. Outside in the hall, Stacy moved her lips silently, pleading with Carter to exonerate himself. She held her breath. She had given him everything, willingly, with both hands and with her heart and soul. There would be nothing left if he failed her now.

Finally Carter let out a long sigh. "Oh, no. Diane, I was hoping this could be avoided."

"Oh, really?" Diane replied frostily.

In the hall, Stacy's heart began pounding wildly. For the second time that night, she was listening in on a conversation she'd give anything *not* to hear.

"Yes." The chair creaked, and Stacy could picture him leaning forward in that intent, serious way he had. "You see, my new lab assistant just called me—she was pretty incoherent, but basically, she said she had stolen a file for me."

He sighed again. "I'm afraid she thought it would help me to have it—I guess she has a little crush on me," he added. "I was hoping I could return the file first thing in the morning and no one would ever be the wiser. I'm sorry it all had to come out, Diane. She's a good kid—I'd hate to see her get into trouble over this."

Another tense silence filled the office. Then Diane Finch spoke again. "I see. What file did she take, Carter?"

"The Maddox Center Studies. I think that's what it was."

There was a rustle of papers, and then the short, sharp slap of a manila folder hitting a desk. "This one, Carter?" Diane asked dryly. "Actually, it never left the building. I think it's rather remarkable that your lab student called you and said she had it."

"Hey, wait a second," the security guard said.

"If it wasn't stolen, how did he know—" The man interrupted himself, as though figuring it all out instantly. "He couldn't have known what file unless he was the one who asked the girl to do it.

"That's how I see it," Diane replied in her cool, detective-like voice. "And now he's trying to make it look like it was all her idea instead of his. Be logical. How on earth would a lab assistant know what file he needed?"

Carter cleared his throat. "This is ridiculous," he said briskly. "There must be some mistake."

"I don't think so. Stacy, come in here," Diane called out.

In a trance, Stacy stepped into the patch of light in the office door. Inside, Carter sat at his desk, staring with a look of growing alarm on his handsome features, while the security guard stood next to him with folded arms and a fierce scowl. Diane Finch stood by the window, staring out into the darkness.

A thin, uncertain smile wavered on Carter's face. "Stacy! Tell them—"

She shook her head. Hot, searing tears welled up behind her lids and blinded her as she stood there, speechless with pain. Diane had said he would throw her to the lions, but it was worse than that, much worse. It had been Diane's research the whole time, and he had lied to her, wooed her into stealing it for him. It was all a lie. Their whole relationship was a lie.

"Stacy—"

With a choking sob, she turned and ran. As she banged the outside door open and stumbled into the night air, a new wave of thunder boomed directly overhead. Stacy drew a shuddering breath as the skies opened up in a flash of lightning. Drenching rain poured down on her, mingling with the stinging tears than rained down her cheeks. With a heartbreaking moan, Stacy sank to her knees in the wet grass and sobbed bitterly into her hands as the storm crashed and roared around her.

Chapter 13

When Stacy opened the door of her suite in Beta House two hours later, she was soaked to the skin. In the living room, Sam, Roni and Maddie were huddled over cups of coffee, and their faces were drawn with anxiety.

"Stacy! Where've you been? You're drenched," Sam cried instantly, setting down her coffee on a pile of magazines. She hurried forward, her hands outstretched to take Stacy in her arms.

Stacy smiled calmly, but gave them an arch, condescending look that halted Sam in her tracks. "I was just out walking," she told them in a steady voice.

"In the pouring rain?" Maddie demanded incredulously.

"Sure. What's wrong with that?" Stacy kicked off her sneakers and peeled off her sopping crew socks. She smiled at them again, but her friends still regarded her apprehensively. "Is something wrong?" she asked politely.

Sam and Roni exchanged puzzled looks, and Maddie shook her head. "We were worried about you, that's all. We found your car keys, so we knew you hadn't driven anywhere. We were just worried," she echoed in a faint voice.

"Well that's sweet of you guys, really," Stacy said as she walked into the bathroom. She came out again rubbing her damp hair with a towel. "But I'm perfectly fine, as you can see." She curled up on the floor and began flipping idly through an old issue of *Vogue* that had been kicking around the suite all summer.

"Are you sure you're okay?" Roni asked slowly. She swirled the dregs of her coffee around for a moment, and then looked into Stacy's eyes again. "Did something happen— you seem sort of—I don't know."

Stacy pursed her lips, considering. Then she shrugged, and gave them an airy laugh. "Actually, you'll all get a kick out of this," she confided, her voice edged with wry amusement.

"Yeah?" Roni prompted.

Lifting herself up on her knees, Stacy reached for Maddie's coffee cup and tipped it toward her to see how much there was. It was half-full. "Can I drink this?" she asked sweetly.

Maddie nodded without speaking.

"Well, anyway," Stacy continued, taking a small sip of coffee. "Remember that stuff about me getting Carter's files and everything? I know you all know about it," she added, giving Roni a knowing grin. Roni blushed in confusion and looked away.

"*Anyway,* it turns out he was just using me to steal Diane Finch's research so he could use it in his proposal. Isn't that just too much?"

There was a stunned silence in the room. Stacy sipped her coffee with an unconcerned manner. With a deep, tired sigh, she leaned back against a chair.

"Stacy, what—what do you mean?" Maddie finally asked.

"It was all an act all along, that's all," Stacy explained. "He was never in love with me, can you believe it?" She let out another nervous laugh. "Just goes to show how conceited I am, thinking every man in the world is ready to fall at my feet."

"No sir," she continued, staring into the coffee cup in her hands. She shook her head slowly, and then looked up with a slightly crooked grin. "But I knew from the beginning what was going on. He really didn't have me fooled for a minute."

Sam stared at her speechlessly, and Maddie cleared her throat. "I thought you were in love with him." she faltered, her blue eyes wide with confusion. "I thought . . ."

"Oh, that!" Stacy twisted her mouth wryly,

and shook her head in a dismissing gesture. "No, not really. Anyway, I'm not going to bother with him anymore. He was getting boring, and now the whole thing is pretty academic since he was caught."

"Caught? How?" Roni asked, her eyebrows drawn together in a worried frown.

"Well—you'll think this is a riot, Ron," Stacy chuckled. "I went to Diane Finch's office again to get another file, and who should walk in and find me but Diane Finch herself? So anyway, we went to Carter's office for a big dramatic showdown, and that's that. The guns are still smoking. I swear," she chuckled. "It was good enough for Broadway."

"When did this happen?" Sam whispered.

"Just a couple of hours ago."

The others looked at Stacy for a minute, then Sam voiced what was clearly on all their minds. "Then where have you been all this time?"

Stacy drained the last of the tepid coffee into her mouth and swallowed. "Just walking around."

"In the rain?"

She raised her eyebrows inquisitively, meeting Sam's astonished gaze. "Yes. It's still about eighty degrees outside. I could hardly catch pneumonia, Sam. I like walking in the rain."

Maddie shifted uncomfortably in her seat. "Are you sure you're okay? I mean, aren't you— a little upset or something?"

"Upset?" Stacy echoed in a surprised tone. "No, why should I be upset?"

Roni let out a gasp of disbelief. "Stacy! For God's sake—wasn't it kind of a shock to find out that guy was *using* you?"

"But I told you, it wasn't a shock," Stacy insisted. "So he really wasn't using me at all."

"You're not upset?" Maddie repeated.

With a short laugh, Stacy rolled her eyes. "Do you guys want to cut up some onions or something so I'll cry—because I guess that's what you expect me to do, right? Break down and cry my eyes out or something?"

The others looked pained. "Stacy," Sam said firmly, crossing to her side and kneeling down next to her. Sam took one of Stacy's hands in her own and looked into her eyes. "Stacy, it just seems a little strange for you to tell us one day you're wildly in love with a guy, and then the next tell us he used you and that it doesn't bother you at all." She shook her head. "Are you sure you aren't just holding it inside?"

"Sam," Stacy began patiently. She squeezed her friend's hand in return and gave her a heartfelt smile. "Sam, you're being very sweet, but honestly, there's nothing to let out! I wasn't really in love with him." She looked at Roni and Maddie and nodded encouragingly. "Really."

She kept smiling at them, trying to convince them. Then she met Roni's eyes.

"What about Pete, then?"

Stacy's nonchalant smile faltered for a fraction of a second. She got up off the floor. "What about him?" She shrugged slightly, and turned toward the bedroom door. "Listen, I've got to change my clothes—I think I'm starting to mildew. And then I'm going for a drive."

"Can I come?" Sam asked quickly. Her cheeks colored as she met Stacy's surprised glance. "Do you mind?"

Stacy looked at Sam for a long moment, and then shifted her gaze to Roni and Maddie. She shook her head, and gave them a cynical, lopsided grin. "Hey, listen. I'm not going to drive over any cliffs or anything. He's definitely not worth it. And besides," she added over her shoulder as she reached for the door handle, "there aren't any cliffs around here that I know of."

With that she slipped into the bedroom and closed the door carefully behind her. Mechanically, she stripped off her damp, mud-stained clothes and stepped into a pair of jeans and dragged a cotton sweater on over her head. She didn't allow herself to think. Then she grabbed her car keys and walked back into the living room with a casual and unhurried gait.

Her friends looked up guiltily as she entered. Obviously they had been discussing her, but Stacy didn't care. They could think whatever they wanted to. She tossed them a light smile. "I'm going to drive around for a while. Don't wait up."

Before they could raise any protests, Stacy

was out the door and running down the stairs. Outside, the air was heavy with moisture even though the rain had stopped. She hurried to her car and ducked inside.

Breathing steadily, she turned on the ignition and pulled away from the curb, keeping her speed well under twenty as she cruised the campus lanes. The headlights sliced through foggy patches and glinted off wet trees and bushes. The campus was quiet and deserted, and Stacy found herself driving aimlessly, turning into side-streets as they appeared.

When she reached the playing fields at the far end of campus, she slowed the car to a stop. The fields stretched away into darkness beyond the headlight's reach. The faint outline of a goalpost was barely visible in the mist. It was on these fields that most of Hawthorne's all-school events were held—rallies, barbecues, rock concerts, and commencement excercises, as well as all the sports meets. Stacy put her head down on the steering wheel, her mind a dead blank.

Sometime later—she didn't know how long she had been there—there was a tap on the window. She raised her head groggily and saw a campus patrolman standing next to her car, flashlight in hand. Beyond him a Hawthorne Security patrol car idled quietly.

She rolled down the window. "Yes?"

The security guard peered at her suspiciously, trying to see inside the car. "Everything okay, young lady? Are you all right?"

The question struck Stacy as ironically appropriate, and she felt a giggle rise in her throat. She knew he probably thought she was drunk or worse, but it didn't matter that much. "No, officer," she said with icy calm. "But I will be. I'm very strong, and I'll get through this."

He raised his eyebrows with even more suspicion.

"I'm not drunk. I'm not stoned. I'm just sitting here thinking. Is that allowed?"

"Hmm." He frowned, and then shrugged. "Well . . . Don't stay here too long. It's late."

Stacy tried to smile, but didn't achieve much more than a faint twist of her lips. "I won't."

With one last look, he turned and climbed back into the patrol car and drove away. Stacy watched the car fade into the mist, but when the last faint glimmer from the headlights disappeared, she felt her whole body sag. She put her head back down on the steering wheel and closed her eyes. She couldn't think about anything now. Tomorrow would come soon enough.

Chapter 14

Stacy pushed open the door of the ceramics studio at nine-thirty the next morning. A summer school pottery class took up one end of the airy room, but her favorite workbench was well-isolated at the other end. She put her head down and slipped into the room, grabbing her clay-stained smock off its hook as she passed. She could ignore a dozen high school students and a teacher easily enough. In fact, she was getting pretty good at blocking certain things out of her mind at will.

For a moment she paused in front of the shelf where she stored her ongoing projects, pushing her arms into the sleeves of her smock. Under a damp cloth, her Tree of Life sculpture was a lumpy, lifeless mass. She hadn't touched it in at least two weeks, and she suspected it might be too dried out at that point to save. She turned away from it and went to the tub of clay with a determined scowl.

The teacher's voice drifted over once in a while, but Stacy tuned it out. Grabbing a handful of dripping wet clay, she hitched herself up on a stool and began wedging it vigorously. The soft clay surrendered to her strong, relentless hands as the previous night's dazed anguish swiftly turned into a burning, overpowering rage.

How could I have been such a fool, Stacy asked herself furiously, doubling the clay over on itself again and again. *How could I have been such a fool?*

As she recalled the cute, sentimental way she had behaved toward Carter, a shudder of mortification and digust racked her body. She thought she would be sick, and swallowed a bitter, acrid taste in her throat.

Her fingers prodded and twisted the clay, her eyes narrowing with concentration. *Well, one thing's for sure*, she added silently. *I'll never fall in love like that again. No way. Nobody's going to catch Stacy Swanson with her guard down again.*

Stacy scooted her stool closer to the workbench, dimly aware of a hollowness in her stomach. Breakfast had been too much to face: she had no appetite for food. And besides, the empty, echoing sensation in her stomach was appropriate: it matched the sensation in her heart perfectly. She knew starving herself wouldn't solve anything, but she simply didn't care.

She walked rigidly to a wheel, and slid onto the seat. With a sarcastic grimace, she slapped the clay down on the wheel. It sat there, a brown, formless lump. Stacy hit the power switch with her foot.

As she wet her hands in the bucket and pressed down on the clay, Stacy admitted cynically that if the story ever came out in Boston, her friends would laugh for a month. She composed a headline in her mind. *The Case of Stacy Swanson: Why Rich Kids Steal.*

"Step right up, folks," she muttered grimly, staring at the whirling clay between her hands. "Step right up and see the laughing stock of Beacon Hill."

A student working nearby cast her a surprised glance. Stacy just scowled even harder and bent over her wheel again. Never again, she repeated to herself, forcing herself not to give way and cry. Her emotions would never betray her again. Never.

The sunshine hit her with its blinding glare as she stepped out onto the steps of the Fine Arts Complex. She fell back a step, dazzled, and put one hand up to shield her eyes.

"Stacy! I've been waiting for you!"

She didn't need to be able to see to recognize the voice. A cold wave of fury clamped down on her. She turned and headed down the steps away from Carter without speaking. She felt sickened by his self-assurance; why would he think she wanted to see him now, after all that had happened?

"Stacy, wait! We need to talk!"

Whirling around, Stacy confronted him squarely, her chest heaving with suppressed indignation. "I don't think we have anything to talk about," she hissed, her voice filled with venom.

Carter looked taken aback by the undisguised hatred in her tone, but his old, charming smile was back in an instant. "Stacy, Stacy," he cajoled. "I know you're upset—"

"Upset?" she repeated, staring at him in amazement.

With a confident, confiding smile, he nodded. "You know I had no choice! I knew they wouldn't come down hard on you—I couldn't take the risk of getting in trouble myself. I did it for us, Stacy. For our future."

"For 'us'?" Stacy laughed and put her hands on her hips. "There is no 'us', Carter. No 'future.' You may have played me for a fool once, but you're wasting your breath now."

"Stacy, you're taking this the wrong way! You don't understand—"

His face fell as she interrupted in a low, menacing tone. "Oh, I understand perfectly. And what's more, if you ever speak to me again, I'll make sure your career is wiped out. I've got friends in high places academically, which I'm sure you were hoping to take advantage of someday. And I certainly won't hesitate to use them. If you aren't finished now, you will be soon. I'll *bury* you."

With that she spun on her heel and stalked away, trembling with pain and anger. She stumbled on the steps of the Dining Commons and caught a faint odor of food. Nauseated, she turned away and headed toward Beta House. The thought of eating lunch was too much: all she could think about was getting in her car and driving away. She didn't want to see anybody or talk to anybody. She just wanted to be alone with her own agonizing thoughts.

Mile after mile sped by under her wheels. Stacy knew she was lost, but she didn't care. She was far out in the countryside, among the low Georgia hills. As far as she could see, there was nothing but red clay, small farms and ramshackle gas stations with old peeling Coca-Cola signs on them.

She stopped at one station for gas and ignored the surprised looks she received from the old men sitting in the shade nearby. Mercedeses weren't very common in Georgia farm country, apparently. And neither were slender, expensively dressed, tired-eyed young women. Her dignity held her up until the car surged away from the station, and then she shook her head wearily.

"What am I doing here, anyway?" she asked out loud. A thin film of red dust had settled on the dashboard, she noticed in a detached way. She shook her head again. "I don't belong here."

I don't belong anywhere, she continued silently. She rested her elbow in the open window and propped her head up on her hand. *I'll just keep driving and driving until I do find someplace I belong. If I ever do.*

With another tired sigh, she switched hands on the steering wheel and reached into the glove compartment. She scattered cassettes onto the seat and floor, irritably looking for one she thought she could bear listening to. She tossed several pop music tapes into the back seat in disgust, and pawed impatiently through the rest. Finally she located her recording of the Bach Brandenburg Concertos, and she slipped it into the tape deck.

Patches of sunlight and shade flashed across the windshield as she sped along the country highway, past telephone poles completely veiled in trailing vines. Stacy's face was set like stone, and even the haunting strains of the perfect, baroque music couldn't move her. She decided she would probably never be able to feel anything again.

Her eyes shifted briefly to the digital clock in the instrument panel: it was after six o'clock in the evening. She had been driving for hours. And she hadn't eaten a thing all day—not that she missed it. But she was bone tired, and wished she could get back to campus so she could go to sleep. She began to look for familiar landmarks, but she didn't hold out much hope.

After a while, a sign saying, "Quarry 4½ Miles" flashed by. Stacy vaguely recalled passing it a few months before on a drive with Pete. A few miles later, she saw a sign for Route 17, the road into Hawthorne Springs, and she breathed a sigh of relief. It wouldn't be much longer. Soon she would be able to crawl into bed and pull the covers over her head.

Without thinking, she turned down the road to Pete's house. Before she knew it, she had rolled to a stop under a tree, and Pete's white, Victorian home was across the road, two houses up.

The angle from where she sat gave her a glimpse of the Youngs' back yard, and she could see that the whole family was gathered there. As usual, it seemed more like a huge family reunion than just one family, but that was just a result of constant movement. The girls and Mrs. Young passed back and forth carrying bowls and dishes of food, while the younger children ran around in some kind of racing game. Beyond the bushes, a thin veil of smoke from a charcoal grill drifted upward. It was easy to picture Pete there with his father, turning hot dogs and chicken legs on the grill with a battered pair of barbecue tongs. They would be talking about sports, or Pete's plans for engineering school, or how to fix one of the twins' go-carts.

Stacy's jaw clenched as she watched the Youngs from her hidden spot. They were so naive. They thought everyone was good and well-meaning and honest. They thought the best of everyone. It would never occur to any of them that there were people in the world who would take advantage of them at a moment's notice. That there were people who would use you if you gave them the chance.

They don't have the slightest idea of what life is really like, Stacy scoffed to herself, folding her arms across her chest. *They don't have a clue. They just keep having cook outs and building their little tree-forts and—*But she choked on her sarcastic words, unable to get them out. Rapidly blinking a tear away, she put the car in gear and drove away down the street. *Where to next?* she thought.

Chapter 15

Stacy spent the next four days in the ceramics studio. It seemed ironic to her that just a week ago she had considered giving up pottery. Now she felt like she might go crazy if she didn't have it. Her shelf was filled with pieces ready to be fired and glazed, although the Tree of Life sculpture was still pushed to the back. Every time she thought about it, she tried to justify letting it go to ruin.

There isn't enough time, she told herself. *I'm leaving for Nantucket the day after tomorrow.*

Nantucket. And Sydney. Ready or not, she had to go spend some time with her mother. Maybe she could be more help to Sydney than either one of them expected, though. They had a lot more in common than either one of them could have known—the same kind of pain, the same brand of betrayal.

She leaned her elbows on the workbench and stared off into space, rubbing at the smudges of dried clay on her hands. The pain was easing up, finally. It was hard to believe it would actually go away completely, but Stacy felt it was getting much easier to bear.

In fact, all she felt now was a dull ache. She knew she had been wildly infatuated with Carter, but it had only lasted a few weeks. Now she had trouble even remembering exactly what Carter looked like. It was beginning to feel like all that had happened in a past life, to a different person. The new Stacy was removed and distant: Nothing could ever hurt her the same way again.

With a thoughtful nod, Stacy pushed herself away from the workbench and wandered to her shelf of finished sculpture. A bar of late afternoon sunlight shot through a high window onto the floor next to her; overhead, the ceiling fan whirred softly. For a moment, a tear trembled on Stacy's eyelashes—it was so peaceful and comforting, it was almost too much.

Then she took a deep breath and reached in the back of the shelf for the Tree of Life.

"I shouldn't even bother," she grumbled as she set the shrouded figure on the table. She perched on the stool and looked at it for a moment. Then she took off the cloth and touched the clay with one finger. It was almost too dried out to work on at all.

She frowned at it objectively, her lips pursed and her arms crossed, and stepped back a pace. Then she reached for a dish of water and some modelling tools, and set to work. With firm, sure strokes, she began paring away at the sculpture, taking it down to the basic lines and forms that gave it definition. All of the built-up, confusing excess disappeared, leaving the pure symbol behind.

She was so deep in thought that she was barely aware that someone was in the room with her. The realization came slowly, until she finally looked up and saw Maddie seated nearby, reading. Her heart turned over, but with gratitude this time.

"Hi."

Maddie raised her eyes quickly, a smile of relief on her lips. "Hi, yourself."

"What are you doing?"

Maddie cocked her head to one side. "Just reading."

"Reading what?"

"*A Tale of Two Cities*," Maddie replied, closing the book on one finger. "Dickens."

Stacy grinned suddenly. "I know it's Dickens. I'm not totally illiterate, thank you."

Her friend returned the smile with a sheepish little shrug, and stood up, putting the book down on her chair. Maddie walked over to Stacy's workbench with a timid smile.

"I'm glad you're working on that," she said, nodding at the Tree of Life. "I always liked it. I was afraid you weren't going to finish it."

Stacy looked at the reshaped, leaner sculpture again. Without warning, tears started rolling down her cheeks and she turned away, embarrassed. Silently, Maddie put one arm across Stacy's shoulder, drawing her toward her. Stacy cried quietly for a few moments, grateful for her friend's unconditional support.

"I guess it really did hurt, huh?" Maddie whispered after a few minutes. "I wish you didn't have to keep it all inside. We just wanted to help you, but well . . ."

Stacy nodded, too moved to say anything. There were times when even she couldn't keep her emotions from getting away from her. And she had to admit that it wasn't always a bad thing.

Sniffing, she walked to the sink and pulled out some paper towels to wipe her eyes. The stiff paper scratched her skin, but at least it soaked up the tears. She stared into the bottom of the big, stained sink and shook her head.

"Thanks, Maddie. I just . . ."

Maddie was silent for a moment. "I understand, Stacy. Really."

"Yeah, well. I'll be okay," she sighed, returning to her work.

They were silent for a few minutes. Every once in a while, Stacy looked up to find her friend's eyes on her, and she managed a small smile each time. At last, the quiet peacefulness of the studio settled in again, and Stacy felt better.

"So, anyway," she began, trying to sound bright and rejuvenated.

Maddie chuckled softly. "Anyway," she sighed. "It's hard to believe summer's nearly over."

"Mmm. I know."

"By the way," Maddie added with a frown. "Have you heard about APA yet? Are you moving in?"

Stacy opened her mouth, surprised. She had completely forgotten about the rooming situation. She had no idea if she had won a room in the APA lottery. Shaking her head, she shrugged with a sad smile. "I don't know, actually."

Thinking about it brought back more bad memories, and Stacy shook her head dejectedly. It was too late to change things with her roommates now. School would be starting in a matter of weeks, and she was leaving in two days. She stared at the clay-covered wooden spatula in her hand.

"I guess I've done enough today," she said wistfully. "I may even be finished, but I can't tell yet."

She soaked the cloth in water again and draped it carefully over the Tree of Life. She reached over and punched Maddie lightly in the shoulder. "Let's get out of here, huh? What do you say?"

Maddie nodded. "Sure."

On the way back to Beta House, they stopped at APA and read the bulletin board. Stacy's name was on the list of sophomores who had managed to land rooms in the sorority.

"Looks like you made it," Maddie said quietly. "Congratulations."

Stacy shrugged. She was too tired to care much one way or the other. At least she had a place to live. "Yeah. I guess so."

They turned down the tree-shaded path to the frat house, walking slowly. "Stacy?"

She looked across at Maddie, who was kicking a pebble as they ambled along. "Yeah?"

"You're still coming to dinner tomorrow night, right? Our farewell celebration? We have reservations at L'Auberge."

Stacy dropped her eyes to the path, not knowing what to say. There seemed to be even less to celebrate than before. The idea of dressing up and going out for a dinner party just made her tired and depressed. She opened her mouth to form an excuse.

But then she thought about Maddie coming so quietly and uncritically to the studio, and the way her roommates had worried about her when she was acting so out of characer. She thought about the smiles of encouragement Sam and Roni had given her over the past few days. They had sensed she needed to work things out by herself, but they had made it clear that they were there if she needed them. She felt a lump rise in her throat.

"Sure, I wouldn't miss it for anything," she whispered. "I'll be there."

On Saturday after lunch, Stacy drove away from campus again. Endless drives in the countryside had become a daily habit she couldn't shake. For all her cynicism, she knew she truly enjoyed the peaceful rolling beauty of the Georgia farmland. She felt deeply moved by the dark mists that crept into the hollows at sunset, and by the stark shapes of pine trees at the sides of the roads. Every weather-stained barn seemed significant, with a strange and profound beauty she had never expected to see.

And now it was her last day in Hawthorne Springs for a while. Even though she knew she would be back in two weeks, she couldn't help feeling like she was at the end of an era, the true end of her freshman year. That night she and her roommates would drink a toast to the year that was over. Things might get better, or they might get worse. But they would never be the same.

In a nostalgic mood, Stacy followed the highway out of town and lost herself in the countryside. But before she had gone too far, she automatically turned the car around and headed for Pete's house. All of her drives took her there eventually. She kept reminding herself that the Youngs were sentimental and naive and unsophisticated—and all the other things she said she despised. But she always felt a little better after looking at their house.

Her car rolled to a quiet stop up the street. She sat there looking at the house, with a tender, melancholy smile on her lips. Suddenly, she felt a loud bump at the rear of the car. Turning quickly in her seat, she found one of Pete's seven-year-old twin brothers—she wasn't sure which one—standing by her window, skate-board in hand.

A flush of embarrassment flooded her cheeks as she rolled her window open.

"Hi, Stacy. Where've ya been?" he yelled. "You haven't been over in *ages*."

"Oh, well . . ." She trailed off. Apparently the younger Youngs didn't know about the way she had treated their adored big brother. And she certainly couldn't bring herself to explain the situation to this eager, sunburned and grass-stained kid. His bright, interested eyes lingered with pure envy on her car, and he wiggled the side-view mirror experimentally.

"Are you coming in?" he continued innocent-ly. He scratched at a Band-Aid on his arm. "Got a cut," he explained in a serious, confidental tone as he noticed her watching him.

"Oh. I'm sorry." Stacy didn't know whether she wanted to laugh or cry.

He dropped his skateboard and popped it up with his foot a few times for practice. "Pete's not home yet, neither are my folks. It's just us."

Stacy stole a quick glance up at the house. An irresistible urge to go into that home one more time pulled at her.

"Come on," he urged again.

"Okay," she said breathlessly, opening her door. "Just for a few minutes, though. I've got packing to do."

Minutes later she was standing in the big, familiar kitchen, surrounded by both twins, Pete's ten-year-old tomboy sister, whom Stacy always thought of as the "Indian" and fifteen-year-old Margaret. She quickly learned that the oldest girl, Alice, was with the baby and their parents, shopping for new lawn furniture. Without much surprise Stacy found herself roped into making up a batch of peanut-butter-and-jelly sandwiches with Margaret.

"We built a greenhouse on our fort," one of the twins said proudly, watching the sandwich production with greedy eyes. "It was Mom's idea—we put a bunch of geraniums in and stuff. And I planted some stuff I found in the woods in pots."

"Quit saying 'stuff'," Margaret whispered, casting Stacy a shy smile.

"Why can't I say 'stuff'?" he retorted hotly, making a grab for a finished sandwich and taking a huge bite. He didn't seem to notice the smear of grape jelly he had left on his cheek. "I like stuff. I like mechanical stuff most. I'm going to be an engineer, same as Pete."

A sharp pang struck Stacy's heart. She concentrated on cutting a sandwich, keeping her eyes lowered until the conversation went veering off in a different, safer direction.

"How's the baby doing?" she asked Margaret. She knew the girl looked up to her, and she always tried to talk to her as an equal. "Is she still trying to stand up—or has she already graduated to riding skateboards?"

The Indian crowed with laughter. "Wouldn't that be a riot? A baby on a skateboard?"

Margaret touched Stacy's arm. "We've got a

new rabbit. We named it Bert. Short for Rab-bert."

For some reason, that set the rest of the kids off in a fresh gale of laughter.

"That's nice," Stacy said, cocking one eye-brow at the children. "But why is that so funny?" She bit into her sandwich. Peanut butter never tasted quite so delicious as it did at the Young's house.

"Well, see, we got Bert and named him Bert—" snorted one of the twins. He cracked up again, unable to finish.

"And then Bert had babies the next day!" finished the other twin, barely containing him-self.

Stacy chuckled. "Sounds like you'll have to change Bert's name to Roberta."

"Or Alberta," Margaret suggested with another shy smile.

"How about Bertina," Stacy went on with a grin. She felt like she was becoming a little too silly, but she didn't care. She took another bite of her sandwich. "Or Zigberta?"

The children erupted into laughter again. In the back of Stacy's mind, her cynical side made a sarcastic observation about how easily amused they were. But Stacy was having too much fun herself to believe that—or care about it, either.

"Or Berticula," she called out amid the bois-terous giggling. "Bertella?" She took another bite, suppressing a giggle, and Pete walked in the back door. Stacy immediately choked on the peanut butter, and started coughing and gasping for breath.

"Stacy's choking!"

"Give her CPR!"

"Pete, do something! Thump her on the back!"

"No—don't whack her, are you crazy?"

Choking and spluttering, Stacy ran to the sink and hastily filled a glass with water. She gulped it down, then coughed for a minute or two. Pete stood frozen in the doorway, watching the scene in a daze.

Stacy knew her face was beet red from the choking coupled with the embarrassment. If she had thought Pete might show up, she never would have risked coming in. She kept her eyes looking down and put her glass in the sink.

"I have to go. Bye," she gasped on a leftover cough. Without another word, she edged past Pete and ran down the back steps.

"Stacy! Hold on!"

She slowed to a halt in the driveway by Pete's truck, but she couldn't bring herself to turn around. Pete's footsteps crunched on the gravel as he walked up behind her. He cleared his throat.

"This is—" He had to clear his throat again. "This is a surprise," he said, his voice strained.

She nodded.

"What are you doing here?"

Turning around, Stacy faced him, meeting his eyes while her cheeks burned. "I—I don't know."

His frank blue eyes narrowed. "Did you want to tell me something?"

"I don't know," she admitted, shaking her head helplessly. She made a futile gesture with her hands. "I honestly don't know."

Nodding thoughtfully, Pete looked down and kicked at a pebble. It skittered down the driveway a few feet while both of them watched it closely.

"I guess," Stacy began uncertainly. Her lips felt dry, and she licked them hurriedly. "I guess maybe I just wanted to—to apologize for—"

Pete was still silent. Stacy felt like a fool, like she was acting selfish and insensitive. Maybe she should just leave, she thought. But she needed to say more. "I'm sorry," she admitted.

A quick blush washed up Pete's throat and cheeks, hiding his freckles.

"I guess I just wanted to say I was an insensitive jerk," she continued harshly. She turned and put her hands on the hood of Pete's pickup truck. "I'm beginning to realize I make a mistake every time I turn around."

Stacy put her head down on her hands on the truck. She was exhausted, and she didn't know what to say or even what she felt. The late afternoon sun filtered through the trees, making dappled patterns on the gravel. It was quiet, and peaceful. Suddenly she knew what she had to say.

"I just don't want to make you hate me, that's all," she finished in a whisper.

"Stacy, I don't—"

She turned and looked at him. Their eyes locked and she held his gaze for a long moment. She could tell he was as bruised on the inside as she was. They weren't about to rush into each other's arms and forget what had happened. Life didn't work that way, Stacy realized sadly.

"I don't hate you, Stacy," he said quietly. He shook his head, his eyes shining with unshed tears. Pressing his lips together, he looked at his house. "But I just—"

"You don't have to say anything, Pete. I didn't mean to—I mean, you don't have to say anything."

He nodded. "I know."

"I shouldn't have even come over," she explained, feeling embarrassed and confused. She looked into his face, picturing a dozen scenes they had shared together. In spite of her decision not to say anything about her feelings, she blurted out, "I missed you."

He nodded again, visibly upset but determined to stay strong. There was nothing secretive or hidden about Pete—whatever he felt or thought, he made clear. In the year she had known him, Stacy had never heard him lie—nor had she seen him trying to live one. He was completely honest about himself.

Letting out a long sigh, she leaned back against the truck and rubbed her eyes tiredly. If only she could be as honest, she thought. She'd lived for so long in a world that depended on subtle lies and the plotting schemes of social politics. But at least she could try.

"I'm leaving for Nantucket tomorrow. I thought it would be nice if, I mean, if it's okay with you we could meet sometime when school starts again. If that's okay."

He swallowed convulsively. "Okay," he breathed. Looking away, he drew a deep, labored breath. "I'll never forget how I felt when you said it was over, though. I can never forget that—"

"I know." Stacy pressed her fist against her chin to keep it from trembling. "We could both use a good friend, though. I know I need all the friends I can get," she added with a tiny laugh. She turned and looked at him evenly. "And I'll be a good one to you if you let me."

He met her eyes again. Tears glistened on his lashes. "Let's just take it slow, then. Okay?"

With a tremendous sigh of relief, Stacy nodded. "That sounds great, Pete."

"One day at a time."

"One day at a time," she echoed, a glimmer of a smile on her lips. "I can't promise I'll never be a jerk again, but I'll try not to be."

He smiled at that, and touched her hand briefly. "I guess that's fair enough."

They smiled at one another, but with wary, cautious smiles. Then Pete let out a deep breath and pushed his sleeves up. "Have a good time in Massachusetts, okay? Y'all come back soon."

"I will," Stacy nodded fervently. "I will."

Chapter 16

"Stacy, which looks better?" Maddie asked, holding up two pairs of shoes. "The black ones or the red ones?"

Turning from the mirror, Stacy looked critically at the shoes, pursing her lips. "With that dress, the red ones."

"Okay. They kill my feet, though. They're unbelievably tight." Maddie leaned over to work the shoes on, adding between gasps, "What am I going to do next year without your fashion advice?"

There was a pause as both girls registered Maddie's remark. Mingled with the excitement of going out was the sadness of breaking up the suite. Tonight was their last night as a foursome.

"I don't know," Stacy replied, trying to keep it light. "You'll just look like a bag lady, I guess."

Maddie giggled. "I guess."

"Come on, you lazy slugs," Roni called out as she sailed in through the door. She was dressed in black harem pants and a gold bandeau top—typical Roni dazzle. She let out a low whistle. "Swanson, are you going in your underwear or *what*?"

Sam giggled as she squeezed through the doorway around Roni. "You know Stacy is never dressed on time. Fashionably late, that's her motto."

Raising her eyebrows with regal disdain, Stacy opened her closet. "You peons," she drawled. "You're so pitifully dim. Art takes time, you know."

Roni and Sam snorted. "Who's Art?" Roni asked sarcastically. "If he's as slow as you, I don't want to meet him."

"Go ahead, I don't care," Stacy continued loftily, trying not to break into a silly grin. "I know it's just jealousy."

"Whooaa!" Maddie and Sam laughed as Roni's expression grew wrathful. "Look out!"

Stacy gave Roni an angelic smile and pulled a pink silk dress from its hanger.

"Not *that* old rag," Roni moaned. "I guess we've only seen you in that thing five million times."

Nodding seriously, Sam asked, "Yeah—didn't you wear that to the Magnolia Festival?"

"*And* the Freshman Parade at Commencement," Roni added with horror.

Maddie sank down on the edge of her bed with a wistful smile. "You guys, I wish we didn't have to split up," she said in a melancholy voice.

An electrifying silence grabbed the other three girls. No one spoke.

Still staring dreamily at the floor, Maddie continued. "I saw a notice on the bulletin board in the administration building. One of the history professors is going on sabbatical and he needs four people to house-sit for him next year. It's right on the edge of campus, one of those pretty brick houses."

Stacy held her breath. She didn't dare say a word. Maddie couldn't be saying this. It wasn't possible! Not after they had all agreed to live apart. It was too late now.

"Oh well," Maddie sighed. "It's just too bad we can't do it."

Slowly, Stacy turned to look at Roni and Sam. They both had stunned expressions on their faces.

Finally Sam exploded. "Why not?" she blurted out, her voice rising into a squeak.

Maddie looked blank. "But you and Roni—"

"But, Stacy—" Roni began.

"No! I thought—" blurted Stacy.

The four girls stared at one another for a second. It was obvious that they each wanted to do it, but no one seemed to know how to say it. Roni was the first one to draw a deep breath and break the freeze.

"Hold on a second here. Stacy, are you saying you'd rather live with us than live at APA?"

Stacy blinked. "You know I would!"

"What?"

"Well, you and Sam seemed so psyched to go off and live by yourselves . . ." She trailed off, her cheeks flaming as she remembered their earlier conversations on the topic. She swallowed hard as she looked at Sam. "I thought you didn't want me."

Sam shook her head vehemently. "We figured you wanted to live at APA so we just decided to make do."

"And we thought Maddie wanted to live alone," Roni added sheepishly.

Maddie looked at them in surprise. "Why would you think that? I was never so happy in my life as when I lived with all of you. I thought everyone realized that!"

Shaking her head in disbelief, Stacy sat down next to Maddie. "We've been running around in circles," she said incredulously. "We were all so worked up about not cramping each other's style that no one said anything!"

Sam swallowed audibly. "Does this mean we would all rather stay together than split up?"

The others exchanged looks and nodded in unison. Sam closed her eyes for a moment, then laughed. "I don't believe this," she giggled. "No—scratch that. With this group, I *do* believe it."

Stacy reached quickly for Maddie's hand.

"Where did you see that sign, Mad?" she demanded. "If it's not too late, we've got to get that house!"

Maddie stared back, her blue eyes wide with anxiety. "But what if it is too late? What'll we do? I'd hate to live by myself now!"

"Don't even think like that," Stacy insisted sternly. Now that they all wanted to stay together after all—they just couldn't split up! It would be too ironic to believe.

Roni swooped down on them, dragging Maddie to her feet. "Yeah. Come on!"

As they were running out the door, Sam paused. "What about our dinner reservations?" she reminded them. She glanced at her watch with a dazed expression and wrinkled her forehead.

Stacy rolled her eyes, and took Sam by the arm. "Don't talk, Sam. Just move."

"Who wants that last slice?" Roni asked, an unmistakable threat in her voice. She smiled sweetly when no one spoke. "Then I guess it's mine."

Stacy giggled as a long, gooey strand of mozzarella stretched from her mouth to her pizza. She broke it off with two fingers and popped it into her mouth. "I'm stuffed. I couldn't eat another slice if my life depended on it."

They were sitting on the floor of the Beta House television room, still dressed in all their finery. Broken furniture, a beer-stained carpet and grafitti-scrawled calendars of girls in swim-suits created the perfect ambiance for their celebration dinner. Empty pizza cartons and dozens of greasy crumbled napkins littered the floor around them, and a jumbo-sized bottle of Diet Coke had rolled under the couch after being emptied.

"Well, all I can say is it's a miracle we caught Professor Buckley just as he was going out," Sam commented. She undid the buckles on one of her sandals, and kicked it off flamboyantly. She gave them a triumphant grin. "And I can't see why there's any reason our living there won't work out. He just has to check our records, and we're in. Period."

Roni snorted. "He better not check my record."

"You mean your academic record, or your criminal record?" Maddie teased.

"Both," Stacy said in a snobby tone, but she smiled warmly at Roni.

"I wish Terry could have been here," Sam went on meditatively. Terry Conklin had lived in their suite first semester, but had left to re-evaluate her life after a near break-down.

"Me, too," Roni admitted. "But if Terry hadn't moved out, we never would have known Miss Madison Lerner."

"A dubious privilege," Maddie giggled.

"Okay, listen you guys," Stacy announced, sitting up on her knees. She noticed a grease spot on her silk dress and made a sour grimace.

Then she shrugged and reached for the bottle of champagne she had bought.

"Time for our toast," she announced, sipping the last drop of soda from her cup.

"Speech! Speech!" Sam called, tapping two plastic forks together. She looked at the forks in disgust when they made only a slight clicking sound and tossed them over her shoulder.

Stacy grinned at her. "I swear, Sam. You're getting a little unbuttoned."

"Just thinking about champagne does that to her," Roni observed. "No self-control, that girl."

"Okay—" Stacy held one hand up for silence, and then struggled with the wire over the cork. "Somebody hold up the cups—this thing is going to blow."

After a brief tussle, she worked the cork out far enough to pop it out with her thumbs. The others winced in anticipation, waiting for the explosion. With a loud *pop*, the cork flew out, and Stacy deftly poured the first overflow into Maddie's cup.

"Madame," she said, offering it to Maddie.

"Mademoiselle," she corrected Stacy. "*Merci*, anyway."

Stacy quickly poured three more cups of champagne and handed them around. "Are we a classy bunch, or what?" she quipped, looking askance at her own paper cup brimming with bubbling wine, tinted only slightly by left-over Coke.

"First toast," Sam said, rising to her knees and

holding her champagne aloft. "To Stacy's trip. May she come home safely to us."

"Hear hear," Maddie agreed. "Don't get eaten by sharks in Nantucket Sound, whatever you do."

Roni sent Stacy an impish grin. "That's right. I don't know what we'd do without your car."

Sticking out her tongue, Stacy threw a balled-up napkin at Roni. "I'll drink to that," she told Sam. She knew she could face whatever Sydney had to dish out, now that she had her friends to come back to. "You three are really the best home I've ever had."

"Uh-oh. I think we're getting dramatic," Roni muttered behind her hand. "Get out the hankies, we're all going to start weeping uncontrollably."

"Shut up, Roni," Stacy said mildly. "Here's another toast. To last year. In spite of everything—"

"In spite of Jon and Aaron," Sam agreed, referring to her two major romances.

"In spite of partying too hard," continued Roni with a shamefaced grin.

"In spite of taking stupid chances," Maddie added softly.

Stacy smiled at her dark-haired friend. "In spite of ourselves, we all pulled through."

They all drank solemnly. "Anybody need a refill yet?" Stacy asked, her eyes sparkling.

"Please," Sam replied with dignity. "Don't insult us."

"Okay." Roni held up her champagne, a serious expression on her face. "I propose a toast to the coming year. I couldn't ask for *no* trouble, because then life would be boring. And I couldn't ask for all A's, because then there'd be nothing to work for," she added with a grin. "All I could ask for is to spend it with three good friends. Because without friends, there'd be nothing at all."

There was a catch in Roni's voice as she finished. The others all smiled, looking at one another without speaking. Then Roni stood up.

"To next year," she said.

Stacy, Sam and Maddie stood up also. "To next year," they echoed.

Together, they drained their cups, and looked at each other seriously again for a minute. Then, in unison, they threw their cups over their shoulders and laughed. "To next year!"